J
Hewett, Anita
  The bull beneath the walnut
tree.

THE BULL BENEATH
THE WALNUT TREE

and other stories

by Anita Hewett

The Bull
Beneath the Walnut Tree
and other stories

Illustrated by Imero Gobbato

McGRAW-HILL BOOK COMPANY
New York · St. Louis · Dallas · San Francisco

CONTENTS

THE BULL BENEATH
THE WALNUT TREE

and other stories

The Bull Beneath
the Walnut Tree

ONCE UPON A TIME there were six little men who went to pick walnuts from a walnut tree.

They climbed up into the great brown branches, and had just started picking the fat round walnuts when they heard a loud snorting and a thudding of hooves, and a big black bull came and stood beneath the tree.

"And here I shall stay," roared the big black bull, "until you come down. And when you come down I shall toss you on my horns. I shall toss you from here into Wednesday week, and you'll never come back, you silly little men."

The six little men looked down at the bull, at his curving white horns and his mean little eyes, and they clung more tightly to the walnut branches. Then nothing could be heard except the creaking of the branches and the snorting breath of the big black bull.

But the first little man was thinking.

"Please, Mr. Bull," he said at last. "The branches are rough and they hurt our hands. We wear brown leather gloves when we come to pick walnuts, but to-day we forgot them. So may we go and fetch them?"

"So you think you can trick me!" roared the big black bull. "If you all go away you won't come back. So *you* can go—alone—you silly little noodle."

Then the first little man climbed down from the tree and went home to their cottage, and when he came back he was carrying six pairs of brown leather gloves.

So the six little men sat in the tree wearing brown leather gloves.

Then nothing could be heard except the rustle of the wind and the snorting breath of the big black bull.

But the second little man was thinking.

"Please, Mr. Bull," he said at last. "The wind is blowing, and our necks are getting cold. We wear knitted woollen scarves when we come to pick walnuts, but today we forgot them. So may we go and fetch them?"

"You can't trick *me*," roared the big black bull. "If you all go away, you won't come back. So *you* can go —alone—you silly little ninny."

Then the second little man climbed down from the tree, and went to their cottage, and he brought back six stripey knitted woolen scarves.

So the six little men sat in the tree wearing brown leather gloves and knitted woollen scarves.

Then nothing could be heard except the patter of rain and the snorting breath of the big black bull.

But the third little man was thinking.

"Please, Mr. Bull," he said at last. "It's raining up here, and our heads are getting wet. We bring our umbrellas when we come to pick walnuts, but today we forgot them. So may we go and fetch them?"

"Trick me, would you?" roared the big black bull. "If you all go away you won't come back. So *you* can go—alone—you silly little muggins."

Then the third little man climbed down from the tree, and went to their cottage, and when he came back he brought six red umbrellas with long black tassels.

So the six little men sat in the tree, wearing brown leather gloves and knitted woollen scarves, with red umbrellas over their heads.

Then nothing could be heard except the sound of coughing, and the snorting breath of the big black bull.

But the fourth little man was thinking.

"Please, Mr. Bull," he said at last. "Don't you hear us coughing? We've all caught cold. We bring cough syrup with us when we come to pick walnuts, but to-day we forgot it. So may we go and fetch it?"

"That's a silly old trick," said the big black bull. "If you all go away, you won't come back. So *you* can go—alone—you silly little noddle."

Then the fourth little man climbed down from the tree and went to their cottage. And when he came back he brought six little bottles of sticky brown cough syrup.

So the six little men sat in the tree wearing brown leather gloves and knitted woollen scarves, with red umbrellas over their heads, drinking from bottles of sticky brown cough syrup.

Then nothing could be heard except the church clock striking, and the snorting breath of the big black bull.

But the fifth little man was thinking.

"Please, Mr. Bull," he said at last. "We've been sitting up in this tree for an hour and a half, and it isn't very comfy on these hard rough branches. We bring little feather cushions when we come to pick walnuts, but today we forgot. So may we go and fetch them?"

"There's never any end to your tricks," roared the bull. "If you all go away you won't come back. So *you* can go—alone—you silly little addlepate."

Then the fifth little man climbed down from the tree and went to their cottage. And when he came back he brought six feather cushions.

So the six little men sat in the tree wearing brown leather gloves and knitted woollen scarves, with red umbrellas over their heads, drinking from bottles of sticky brown cough syrup, sitting on six little soft feather cushions.

Then nothing could be heard except the sound of groaning, and the snorting breath of the big black bull.

But the sixth little man was thinking.

"Please, Mr. Bull," he said at last. "Don't you hear us groaning? We're groaning with hunger. We bring sandwiches with us when we come to pick walnuts, but today we forgot. So may we go and fetch them?"

"It's the last trick you'll try," roared the big black bull. "If you all go away, you won't come back. So *you* can go—alone—you silly little ninnyhammer."

Then the sixth little man climbed down from the tree and went to their cottage. And when he came back he brought six beef sandwiches with just a little mustard and a great deal of pepper.

So the six little men sat in the tree wearing brown leather gloves and knitted woollen scarves, with red umbrellas over their heads, drinking from bottles of sticky brown cough syrup, sitting on six little soft feather cushions, eating beef and pepper sandwiches.

Then nothing could be heard except the sound of sneezing.

"There's—atishoo—too much pepper," said the six little men. And they sneezed without ceasing till the branches shook and shivered and the walnuts fell plopping down all around the tree.

"You silly little men," said the big black bull. "You'll sneeze yourselves out of the tree before long."

And the big black bull was absolutely right.

The first little man sneezed out of the tree, and as the bull bellowed, the first little man popped the brown leather gloves on the bull's sharp horns.

The second little man sneezed out of the tree, and as the bull bellowed, the second little man tied his knitted woollen scarf around the bull's thick neck.

The third little man sneezed out of the tree, and as the bull bellowed, the third little man fixed his red umbrella to the bull's thrashing tail.

The fourth little man sneezed out of the tree and as the bull bellowed, the fourth little man tipped cough syrup over the bull's tossing head.

The fifth little man sneezed out of the tree, and as the bull bellowed, the fifth little man shook out the feathers from his little feather cushion and they stuck to the syrup on the bull's angry face.

Then the sixth little man sneezed out of the tree, and as the bull bellowed, the sixth little man popped his beef and pepper sandwich in the bull's open mouth.

Then the big black bull couldn't bellow any more, with the gloves on his horns, and the scarf around his neck, the umbrella on his tail, and his face full of feathers. He spat out the sandwich, but it wasn't any use. He sneezed and he sneezed till he sneezed himself helpless.

Then the six little men went home to their cottage. They locked the door, and made soup for their supper.

The bull beneath the walnut tree went on sneezing. And when he had sneezed for an hour and a half, he went away. And he never came back.

The Singing Witch

ONCE UPON A TIME a great gray castle stood on a hill near the edge of a forest. At the foot of the hill ran a silvery stream with a narrow wooden bridge across it.

A wicked witch lived in the castle. She was ragged as a scarecrow, and old and ugly, but one thing about her was beautiful and sweet. Every day as the sun came up she sang a song which was so enchanting that the birds in the trees stopped singing to listen.

But the beautiful song was a wicked trap for anyone who wandered in the forest at sunrise. It drew them toward the great gray castle until they reached the silvery stream, and as soon as they crossed the wooden bridge they were changed into ravens. There was only one way to break the spell. If someone sang a more beautiful song than the one the witch sang every sunrise, then her power would be gone, and the sad, croaking ravens would turn into human beings again. But it seemed that the witch would sing forever, because no one could match her enchanting song.

In a cottage on the other side of the forest lived five brothers and their young sister Isobel. Isobel was happy living in the cottage. She kept it as clean as a bright new pin, and when the brothers came home from work there was always a good meal ready on the table. The brothers loved their pretty young sister, and every day before they left the cottage they warned her to keep away from the castle. "Remember the wicked witch," they said. "Never, never cross the narrow wooden bridge. If you do, we shall never see you again."

Isobel loved to wander in the forest, but she kept

away from the silvery stream, and the castle where the sad black ravens croaked. Week followed week, the hard winter passed, and spring brought fresh green leaves to the trees. One evening Isobel sat by the window gazing up at the darkening sky, and she suddenly remembered that tomorrow was May Day, and also the birthday of her youngest brother, John. She sighed to herself, "I have nothing to give him."

And then, as the stars came out, she smiled. "I shall give him flowers," she said to herself. "The forest is full of flowers in the springtime. I shall get up early, before sunrise, and search in the farthest parts of the forest for bluebells and violets and little white windflowers."

Next morning, as soon as the sky began to lighten, Isobel crept from the cottage very quietly, so as not to awaken her five sleeping brothers.

The bluebells were easy to find. They were everywhere. Then Isobel found some tiny purple violets. "But where are the little white windflowers?" she said. She wandered further into the forest, searching for the little white flowers that she wanted. And just before sunrise she came to the stream. Isobel stopped by the narrow wooden bridge and looked across at the great gray castle. And there, on the other side of the stream, little white windflowers were growing.

Isobel sighed. "I mustn't cross the bridge. I promised never to cross it," she said. "But it wouldn't take a moment to pick the flowers."

Isobel put one foot on the bridge. Then quickly she began to run across it. And when she was nearly halfway across, the red sun rose, and out from the castle came the beautiful sound of the witch's song. Isobel tried to run back to the forest, but the song drew her on to the end of the bridge, and as she set foot on the other side, the flowers fell from her arms to the ground, and among them was a small, black, croaking raven.

When Isobel's brothers found that she had gone, they searched in the forest, calling her name. At last they came to the silvery stream. They looked across it to the great gray castle and saw dying flowers scattered on the ground, and farther away, on the castle wall, a small black raven that croaked very sadly.

At first the brothers were in despair.

"We shall never see Isobel again," they said.

But Michael, the eldest, spoke bravely to his brothers.

"We must break the witch's spell," he said. "We must search the world for a song even lovelier than the one the witch sings every sunrise.

Michael went first to search for a song. He traveled for several days and nights along the wide road that led to the sea, and at last he came to a little harbor where fishermen sat and mended their nets. The sun was going down on the rim of the sea, and Michael stopped to rest for a moment. And then the fishermen started to sing. Their song was quiet, like little waves breaking.

"I have never heard anything more beautiful," said Michael. And when the fishermen ended their song he told them about the witch, and Isobel, and then he led them to the silvery stream. As soon as the sun began to rise the fishermen started to sing their song. But out of the castle came the witch's song, and the fishermen's voices faded away, and their faces were suddenly gray and old.

Then the second brother, Peter, went to search for a song. He traveled for several days and nights until he came to a little village. It was growing dark, and Peter stopped to rest. The door of one of the cottages was open, and inside was a mother singing to her baby. The lullaby was gentle, like a little shower of rain.

"I have never heard anything more beautiful," said Peter, and when the mother had finished singing he told her about the witch's spell. And then he led her to the silvery stream. As soon as the sun began to rise she started to sing her gentle song. But out of the castle came the witch's song, and the gentle lullaby died away as the baby puckered its face and cried.

Then the third brother, Gabriel, searched for a song. He traveled for several days and nights until he came to a strange, wild country, high above the sea where the wild winds blew. He stopped to rest near some twisted trees, where some gypsies had camped with their caravan. And then the gypsies began to sing, and their song was as strange and wild as the wind.

"I have never heard anything more beautiful," said Gabriel, and when the gypsies had finished their song he told them about the sad black ravens. And then he led them to the silvery stream. As soon as the sun began to rise the gypsies sang their strange wild song. But out of the castle came the witch's song, and the gypsies bowed their heads and were silent.

Then the fourth brother, Martin, searched for a song. He traveled for several days and nights and at last he came to a wonderful palace. Around the palace were magnificent gardens, with flowers and trees and smooth green lawns. It was nearly nighttime, and Martin stopped to rest. As the stars came out, a nightingale sang. Its song was cool and clear as a stream, and warm as sunshine, and radiant as the moon.

"I have never heard anything more beautiful," said Martin. He took the nightingale gently in his hand, and traveled back to the silvery stream. As soon as the sun began to rise, the nightingale sang its beautiful song. But out of the castle came the witch's song, and the nightingale drooped its head and stopped singing.

Then the youngest brother, John, went in search of a song.

"It is useless," said his brothers. "The spell will not be broken. If you search and search in the whole wide world you will never find a more beautiful song than the one the witch sings every sunrise."

But John set out bravely and traveled many miles. At last he came to a lonely country where great black mountains towered to the sky. "Shall I find a song here?" John asked himself sadly. "I must go on farther, I must search the whole world. I *must* save Isobel. I *must* break the spell."

Then came back the echo of his voice from the mountains. "Must save Isobel. Must break the spell."

John went no farther. He turned around, and traveled back to the silvery stream. Then he began to build a wall. Stone by stone he built it up, a long gray wall, strong and tall. He worked for seven days to build it, and then he went to tell his brothers.

"Come to the silvery stream," he said. "And then you will see what will happen at sunrise."

All night long the brothers waited, standing by the stream near the narrow wooden bridge. Then the sky grew lighter and the sun began to rise. Out of the castle came the witch's song, and it seemed that nothing could match it for beauty. Then back came the echo of her song from the wall. And the sound of the echo in the clear morning air was even more lovely than the song itself.

The witch's song changed to an ugly croak as the spell was broken, and out of the castle came all the people who had been set free. Among them was Isobel, with flowers in her arms. She went to her brothers, laughing as she ran. And then she turned to John, and gave him the flowers, bluebells and violets and little white windflowers.

So at last the great gray castle was silent, and the witch's power was gone forever. And high against the sky, on the castle wall, one black raven flapped its ragged wings.

Fred

FOR TWENTY YEARS Frederick Penny-feather-Wooderson-Williams saved up his money. And with this money he bought a shop—a grocer's shop in the middle of a village.

Then Frederick Pennyfeather - Wooderson - Williams said to his wife, "Just you see, Maria. We'll make a fortune. Just you see!"

"What will you call the shop?" asked Maria, as she dusted the shelves and tidied the tins.

Frederick Pennyfeather - Wooderson - Williams thought for a moment and then he said: "What's the name of the fishmonger next to us, dear?"

"Albert Fitz-Adams," said Maria. "Very grand!"

"And the chemist next door on the other side?"

"John Hyde-Edwards," said Maria. "*Very* grand!"

Frederick Pennyfeather-Wooderson-Williams said, "We must be grand as well, Maria. I shall put *my* name up over the shop."

Maria said, "Now, look here, Fred Williams, it's much too long, as you very well know."

But Frederick Pennyfeather-Wooderson-Williams sent for a signwriter straight away. The signwriter came with a ladder, paint, and brushes, and he looked at the space where the name was to be, and he looked at the name to go in the space.

"Can't be done!" he said to himself. Then he opened his paint tin, and climbed the ladder, and started to paint a big black F.

Three hours later he came down the ladder, stepped back, and looked up.

"Honest, I did my best," he said.

In tall black letters, the name above the shop said:
FREDERICK PENNYFEATHER-WOODERSON-WILL.

"Will *what?*" said Maria. "I told you so, Fred Williams."

Frederick Pennyfeather - Wooderson - Williams wouldn't be beaten. He went to the printer.

"I want white paper bags in three sizes," he said. "And I want you to print in neat green letters: 'Provisions and Groceries. Orders Delivered. Frederick Pennyfeather-Wooderson-Williams.'"

"Can't be done," said the printer right away. "You'll have to make a choice, I'm telling you straight. Either very big bags with middle-size letters, or middle-size bags with very small letters. Oh well! I can try, if you've made up your mind."

Three days later the paper bags were ready.

"Honest, I tried to oblige," said the printer.

The name on the bags said, in neat green letters: "Provisions and Groceries. Orders Delivered. FREDERICK PENNYFEATHER-WOOD."

"Would if you could, I suppose," said Maria.

But Frederick Pennyfeather-Wooderson-Williams wouldn't be beaten. He bought a little van. Then he drove it to the garage, and he said to the garage man,

27

"I want big red letters on the side of my van. 'Provisions and Groceries. Orders Delivered. Frederick Pennyfeather-Wooderson-Williams.'"

"Can't be done big *that* long," said the garage man. "Oh! All right, if you say so, I'll try."

Six days later the garage man said, "I could tell from the start that it couldn't be done."

The name on the van said, in big red letters: "Provisions and Groceries. Orders Delivered. FREDERICK PENNYFEAT."

"So the van must go back to the garage," said Maria. "It's your feet you'll be walking on, Frederick Pennyfeat."

Frederick Pennyfeather-Wooderson-Williams had a good hard think. Then he went to the signwriter. After that he went to the printer. And then he talked to the garage man.

Three days later there were just four letters—great shiny black ones—over the shop. They said FRED.

FRED said the paper bags, in three different sizes.

FRED said the shining red letters on the van. You could see them quite clearly from half a mile away.

"Let's go to Fred's for some lollipops," said the children.

"Popping down to Fred's for some biscuits," said the mothers.

"Going along to Fred's for a chat," said the fathers.

Frederick Pennyfeather - Wooderson - Williams made a fortune with his shop.

"You're a marvel," said Maria. "I knew it all along, so there, Fred Williams!"

Calamity!

On monday morning Mrs. McConaghie looked from her window and saw a little mouse. He was walking down the lane at the bottom of her garden.

"He'll eat up my strawberries," said Mrs. Mc-Conaghie. "And *that* won't do."

So she had a fence built at the bottom of the garden, to keep the mouse out of the strawberry patch.

"There!" she said. "There! That's better. In a few more days the strawberries will ripen, and I'll have them with cream for my tea on Sunday."

But the little gray mouse made a hole in the fence.

On Tuesday morning Mrs. McConaghie looked from her window and what did she see? The little gray mouse in the strawberry patch! Mrs. McConaghie picked up her dish mop and ran at the mouse, but he stayed where he was. Then Mrs. McConaghie called, "Calamity!

Misery, misery, mercy me!
I look from my window and what do I see?
Will nobody help an old woman to catch
The little gray mouse in the strawberry patch?"

Then a voice from the other side of the fence said, "Yes, I'll help you, Mrs. McConaghie. I'm the spitting black cat that lives down the lane. Make a cat-sized hole in your tall wooden fence, and then I'll come in and I'll chase out the mouse."

So the cat came in and spat at the mouse and chased it away through the mouse-sized hole.

"Well, that's better," said Mrs. McConaghie.

"Now I'll have strawberries and cream on Sunday."

But on Wednesday morning Mrs. McConaghie looked from her window and what did she see? The spitting black cat in the strawberry patch! Mrs. McConaghie picked up a ladle and ran at the cat, but the cat sat tight. Then Mrs. McConaghie called, "Calamity!

Misery, misery, mercy me!
I look from my window and what do I see?
Will nobody help an old woman to catch
The spitting black cat in the strawberry patch?"

Then a voice from the other side of the fence said, "Yes, I'll help you, Mrs. McConaghie. I'm the barking white dog from the butcher's shop. Make a dog-sized hole in your tall wooden fence, and then I'll come in and I'll chase out the cat."

So the dog came in and barked at the cat, and chased it away through the cat-sized hole.

"And a good job, too," said Mrs. McConaghie. "Now I'll have strawberries and cream on Sunday."

But on Thursday morning Mrs. McConaghie looked from her window and what did she see? The barking white dog in the strawberry patch! Mrs. McConaghie picked up a broom and ran at the dog. But the dog didn't care. Then Mrs. McConaghie called, "Calamity!

Misery, misery, mercy me!
I look from my window and what do I see?
Will nobody help an old woman to catch
The barking white dog in the strawberry patch?"

Then a voice from the other side of the fence said, "Yes, I'll help you, Mrs. McConaghie. I'm the hissing gray goose from the farm in the valley. Make a goose-sized hole in your tall wooden fence, and then I'll come in and I'll chase out the dog."

So the goose came in and hissed at the dog, and chased him away through the dog-sized hole.

"And that settles *him*," said Mrs. McConaghie. "Now I'll have strawberries and cream on Sunday."

But on Friday morning Mrs. McConaghie looked from her window and what did she see? The hissing gray goose in the strawberry patch! Mrs. McConaghie picked up a clothes prop and ran at the goose. But the goose stayed put. Then Mrs. McConaghie called, "Calamity!

Misery, misery, mercy me!
I look from my window and what do I see?
Will nobody help an old woman to catch
The hissing gray goose in the strawberry patch?"

Then a voice from the other side of the fence said, "Yes, I'll help you, Mrs. McConaghie. I'm the butting old goat from Long Acre Meadow. Make a goat-sized hole in your tall wooden fence, and then I'll come in and I'll chase out the goose."

So the goat came in and butted the goose, and chased it away through the goose-sized hole.

"And not before time," said Mrs. McConaghie. "Now I'll have strawberries and cream on Sunday."

But on Saturday morning Mrs. McConaghie looked from her window and what did she see? The butting old goat in the strawberry patch! Mrs. McConaghie picked up a rake and ran at the goat. But the goat wouldn't budge. Then Mrs. McConaghie called, "Calamity!

Misery, misery, mercy me!
I look from my window and what do I see?
Will nobody help an old woman to catch
The butting old goat in the strawberry patch?"

Then a voice from the other side of the fence said, "Yes, I'll help you, Mrs. McConaghie. I'm the bellowing bull from over the hill. Make a bull-sized hole in your tall wooden fence, and then I'll come in and I'll chase out the goat."

So the bull came in and bellowed at the goat, and chased it away through the goat-sized hole.

"Not a moment too soon," said Mrs. McConaghie. "Now I'll have strawberries and cream on Sunday."

But on Sunday morning Mrs. McConaghie looked from her window and what did she see? The bellowing bull in the strawberry patch!

Mrs. McConaghie picked up a spade and ran at the bull. But the bull tossed his horns. Then Mrs. McConaghie called, "Calamity!

Misery, misery, mercy me!
I look from my window and what do I see?
Will nobody help an old woman to catch
The bellowing bull in the strawberry patch?"

Then a voice from the other side of the fence said, "Yes, I'll help you, Mrs. McConaghie. I'm the lonely old man from the tumbledown cottage. Make a man-sized hole in your tall wooden fence, and then I'll come in and I'll chase out the bull."

So the man came in and ran at the bull and chased it away through the bull-sized hole.

"I'm glad you came," said Mrs. McConaghie. "Won't you stay to tea? I'm having strawberries and and cream."

So they picked the strawberries and had them for tea, with Devonshire cream and sugar cubes.

On Monday morning the lonely old man came back with a tin full of nails, and a hammer. And he mended the holes in the tall wooden fence.

"I couldn't have done it," said Mrs. McConaghie. "It's hard—being a widow and all alone."

"I'm alone, too," said the lonely old man. "So let's get married, Mrs. McConaghie."

From that day forward there were no more calamities. And, together, they tended the strawberry patch.

The Tiger in the Tent

ONE FINE DAY in the middle of April, two little men called Shuffty and Muffty made up their minds to go camping together. They collected all the things they would need, and packed them into a little old handcart.

"There's the tent," said Shuffty. "And our sleeping

bags, and two warm blankets in case there's a frost. The stripey red and black one is mine, because I like it."

"The black and yellow stripey one is mine," said Muffty.

"There are two pork pies in the hamper," said Shuffty. "And a chocolate cake with walnuts in it. And a small sliced loaf for making sandwiches. And a big tin of honey and a quarter pound of ham. I'll have the honey. I like honey sandwiches."

"I'll have the quarter pound of ham," said Muffty.

"There's a gun and a fishing rod," Shuffty said. "The rod is mine. I'm good at fishing."

"The gun is mine," said Muffty. "Bang bang!"

Then the two little men set off to go camping. They pitched their tent at the bottom of a hill, halfway between a forest and a river. And just as the sun set behind the forest trees, Shuffty and Muffty ate their pork pies, and got into their sleeping bags and went to sleep.

The two little men slept soundly all night, and when they woke up the sun was rising and the water in the river had golden ripples.

"I'm glad there wasn't a frost," said Shuffty.

"So we didn't need our blankets after all," said Muffty.

Then Shuffty opened the tin of honey, and Muffty got out the ham and the bread.

"I'm going fishing by the river," said Shuffty, as he made his second honey sandwich.

"And I'm going hunting in the forest," said Muffty. He made his fourth and last ham sandwich and put them all in a paper bag. Then he took his gun and his packet of sandwiches and set off up the hill to the forest.

Honey sandwiches were difficult to make, and Shuffty was sticky by the time he had finished. And just as he reached for a paper bag, Muffty's gun went *bang!* in the forest. Shuffty jumped, and upset the honey, and it trickled all over Muffty's blanket.

Shuffty picked up the sticky blanket and took it to the river and washed it clean. Then he went back to the camping ground, and hung the black and yellow striped blanket on a line across the door of the tent. Then at last he went to the river to fish. All day long Shuffty fished, and at one o'clock he ate his honey sandwiches. He caught nine little fish, but he didn't know their names.

Muffty hunted in the forest all day, and at one o'clock he ate his ham sandwiches. He shot three black rats and eleven fir cones.

The birds were nearly asleep in the trees when

Muffty went back to the camping ground. The sky in the west was pink and yellow, and long gray shadows lay across the ground. Muffty stopped at the top of the hill beside the gray-green trunk of a pine tree, and he looked down the hill to the camping ground.

And there, in the door of the tent, was a tiger!

Muffty couldn't see its eyes, but he saw its black and yellow stripes. And whenever the wind blew, the tiger moved.

"It's a tiger all right—a big one," said Muffty. "So I can't go back to the tent, that's certain. Not until I've frightened that tiger away. I must think of a frightening tiger thing, a terrible tiger-frightening thing."

Then Muffty walked twice round the pine tree— thinking. And as he walked he said to himself:

"A tiger is frightened of . . .
A tiger is frightened of . . .
Hunters!"

So Muffty made his face look fierce, and he took his gun and ran down the hill making hunting noises.

"*Wheep-wheep-bang!* Shoo you old tiger! *Weep-wheep-bang!*"

But the tiger just sat there, not frightened at all,

and his black and yellow stripes looked fiercer than
ever. So Muffty did a very speedy right-about turn,
and scuttled back quickly to the top of the hill. Then
he walked round the pine tree three times—thinking.

"A tiger is frightened of . . .
A tiger is frightened of . . .
A tiger is frightened of . . .
Red Indians!"

So Muffty borrowed two extra long feathers from one of the pigeons that lived in the tree. He stuck the feathers behind his ears and ran down the hill making Indian noises.

"Wah-wah-woollah-woollah. Wah-wah-woollah-woollah. Me Chief Muffty. Wah-wah-woollah-woollah."

But the tiger just sat there, not frightened at all, and now he seemed to be bigger than ever.

So Muffty did a very speedy right-about turn, and scuttled back quickly to the top of the hill. Then he walked round the pine tree four times, thinking.

"A tiger is frightened of . . .
A tiger is frightened of . . .
A tiger is frightened of . . .
A tiger is frightened of . . .
A Thing he doesn't know about."

So Muffty took the paper bag that had held his four ham sandwiches, and he put it over his head like a hood. He made two little holes in the front for his eyes, and two little holes at the sides for his ears. Then he ran down the hill making strange loud noises.

"Gong-gonk, stidder-pop, ho hi ho!"

But the tiger just sat there, not frightened at all. There were thunder clouds now, beyond the river, and it seemed as though the tiger growled. Muffty did a very speedy right-about turn, and scuttled back quickly to the top of the hill. He was just about to walk round the pine tree again, when he looked toward the river and saw Shuffty coming. Shuffty was carrying nine little fish, and making his way to the camping ground. And because he was coming from the other direction, he couldn't see the tiger in the door of the tent.

Muffty bounced up and down, and shouted, "Keep away, Shuffty. There's a tiger in the tent. He'll eat you, Shuffty. There's a tiger in the tent."

But thunder growled loudly across the sky, and Muffty's voice was lost in the noise. Shuffty came nearer and nearer to the tent, right to the back of it, and then round the side. Muffty could hardly bear to look. He was sure that the tiger would pounce on Shuffty and gobble him up in one big bite.

Then Shuffty came to the door of the tent, and

. . . he took hold of the tiger and folded it up.

Muffty walked round the pine tree, thinking.

"Black and yellow stripes . . .
Black and yellow stripes . . .
Yellow stripes and black . . .
Yellow stripes and black . . .
When is a tiger *not* a tiger?"

After five times round he knew the answer. And he walked down the hill and into the tent.

"Hello, Shuffty."

"Hello, Muffty. I caught nine little fish, but I don't know their names."

"I shot three black rats and . . . an elephant," said Muffty. "Why did you hang up my black and yellow blanket?"

"Why, to keep out the draft, of course," said Shuffty.

Then the two little men ate their chocolate cake for supper, and got into their sleeping bags and went to sleep.

The Little
White Singing Bird

THERE WAS ONCE a princess who lived in a palace, and outside her window a rose tree grew. It had tiny curving thorns and strong glossy leaves, and little green buds that were closed up tightly. As soon as the sun began to shine, the buds unfolded their silky petals and the tree was covered with golden yellow roses.

Then a little white singing bird came to the tree and sang among the roses all day long. The princess leaned from her window to listen, and she grew to love the little white singing bird.

But a gray day came when the bird flew away. The princess leaned from her window calling, calling to the little white bird to come back. All day long her eyes searched the sky, watching for the flutter of small white wings. But the sky was cold and dark and empty.

Then the golden yellow petals of the roses faded. And as they faded, day by day the sad princess grew paler and paler.

Then the golden yellow petals were flecked with brown, and the roses drooped on their delicate stems. And the sad princess sat quiet and still, staring down at the dry gray earth.

Then one by one the rose petals fell, dropping silently onto the ground. And the princess looked from her window and wept.

"She will die," said the king, "as the rose tree dies. Find the little white singing bird. Then roses will grow again on the tree. It will live, and so my daughter will live."

But the little white singing bird was nowhere to be found, though many men searched for many days. And as day followed day the rose tree withered, and the princess neither smiled nor spoke.

In a cottage near the forest lived four brothers—Roland, Robert, Daniel and David. And when they heard how the sad princess sat weeping by her window day after day they decided to search for the little white bird.

"I shall go to the forest," said Roland, the eldest. "And there I shall find the little white bird, high in the branches of the tallest tree."

On his way to the forest he came to a garden where a ragged old woman stood by the gate.

"Help an old woman," she called to Roland. "Help me to plant this little brown seed."

But Roland refused to help the old woman.

"I am on my way to the forest," he said. "I must find the little white singing bird and save the life of the sad princess. How can I stay to help an old woman?"

Then Roland went to the wide green forest and searched in the branches of the tallest trees. But although he searched for seven days the little white singing bird was nowhere to be found. So Roland caught a blue-feathered dove and carried it gently in his hands to the palace, where he set it in the dying branches of the rose tree. The dove called softly, *roo-coo roo-coo*, and the last of the rose petals fell to the ground. And the princess wept bitterly.

Then it was Robert's turn to search.

"I shall go through the wide green forest," he said. "And farther still to the edge of the sea. And there, where the sea-foam breaks on the rocks, I shall find the little white singing bird."

On his way to the sea he came to the garden where the ragged old woman stood by the gate.

"Help an old woman," she called to Robert. "Help me to plant this little brown seed."

Robert was anxious to go on his way, but when he looked at the ragged old woman and saw that her fingers were stiff and twisted, he took the little brown seed from her hand and planted it deep in the stony earth.

And out of the seed, in less than a minute, grew a tall yellow weed.

"Help me once more," said the ragged old woman. "Help me to pull up this tall yellow weed and throw it down on the rubbish heap."

But Robert refused to help the old woman.

"I am on my way to the sea," he said. "I must find
the little white singing bird and save the life of the
sad princess. How can I stay to help an old woman?"
Then Robert went on through the wide green for-

est, and further still to the edge of the sea. And there, where the sea-foam broke on the rocks, he searched for the little white singing bird. But although he searched for seven days, the little white singing bird was nowhere to be found.

So Robert caught a gray-feathered gull, and carried it gently in his hands to the palace, where he set it in the dying branches of the rose tree. The gull called sadly with its lost, wailing cry, and the branches of the rose tree withered a little. And the princess wept more bitterly than ever.

Then it was Daniel's turn to search.

"I shall go through the wide green forest," he said. "And farther still to the edge of the sea. I shall cross the sea to a faraway country where the sun shines brightly day after day. And there, on the banks of a great green river, I shall find the little white singing bird."

On his way to the river he came to the garden where the ragged old woman stood by the gate.

"Help an old woman," she called to Daniel. "Help me to plant this little brown seed."

Daniel looked at the ragged old woman and saw that her fingers were stiff and twisted, so he took the little brown seed from her hand and planted it deep in the stony earth. And out of the seed, in less than a minute, grew a tall yellow weed.

"Help me once more," said the ragged old woman. "Help me to pull up this tall yellow weed and throw it down on the rubbish heap."

Daniel was anxious to go on his way, but when he looked at the ragged old woman and saw the weary droop of her shoulders, he pulled the tall yellow weed from the ground and threw it down on the rubbish heap. In less than a minute a thorn bush grew, and on one of its branches was a little white flower. The little white flower faded and died, and where it had blossomed was a round red berry.

"Help me once more," said the ragged old woman. "Help me to plant this round red berry in the cool damp earth by the edge of the stream."

But Daniel refused to help the old woman.

"I am going to a great green river," he said. "I must find the little white singing bird and save the life of the sad princess. How can I stay to help an old woman?"

Then Daniel went on through the wide green forest, and farther still to the edge of the sea. Then he crossed the sea to the faraway country where the sun shone brightly day after day. And there, on the banks of the great green river, he searched for the little white singing bird. But although he searched for seven days, the little white singing bird was nowhere to be found.

So Daniel caught a red-feathered parrot and brought it back in his hands to the palace, where he set it in the dying branches of the rose tree. The parrot called loudly with its harsh angry cry, and the tiny curving thorns on the rose tree shriveled. Then the sad princess was too distressed to weep. She lay still and pale, and it seemed that she would die.

Then it was David's turn to search. But his three elder brothers said, "What is the use? We have searched in the forest, at the edge of the sea, and far away by the great green river. You are young, just a boy, so what do you know of the wide world and all that is in it?"

But David would not listen to his elder brothers.

"I shall go where I must and do what I must, and that is all I know," he said.

Before very long he came to the garden where the ragged old woman stood by the gate.

"Help an old woman," she called to David. "Help me to plant this little brown seed."

David looked at the ragged old woman and saw that her hands were stiff and twisted, so he took the little brown seed from her hand and planted it deep in the stony earth. And out of the seed, in less than a minute, grew a tall yellow weed.

"Help me once more," said the ragged old woman. "Help me to pull up this tall yellow weed and throw it down on the rubbish heap."

David looked at the ragged old woman and saw the weary droop of her shoulders, so he pulled the tall yellow weed from the ground and threw it down on the rubbish heap. In less than a minute a thorn bush grew, and on one of its branches was a little white flower. The little white flower faded and died, and where it had blossomed was a round red berry.

"Help me once more," said the ragged old woman. "Help me to plant this round red berry in the cool damp earth by the edge of the stream."

David looked at the ragged old woman and saw the sadness in her tired old eyes. So he took the round red berry from the thorn bush and planted it close to the edge of the stream.

In less than a minute a small tree grew, with delicate leaves on its curving branches. On the topmost branch grew a big blue flower, as bright and lovely and glowing with color as all the joy in the whole wide world.

Then away in the paler blue of the sky came a flutter of small white wings. And the little white singing bird came to the tree and sang its song to the lovely blue flower.

David took the little white bird and carried it gently in his hands to the palace, where he set it in the dying branches of the rose tree. The little white bird was silent for a moment, then it lifted its head and sang to the sky. The notes of its song rose and fell, very softly, as fresh and gentle as a shower of rain. Then tiny shoots appeared on the rose tree, and fresh green stems grew straight and true. Tender curving thorns grew, and strong glossy leaves, and little green buds that were closed up tightly.

"The rose tree lives," said the king. "It lives, and so the princess my daughter will live."

But the princess still lay pale and sad, believing that the song she heard was a dream. Then the king led David to the sad princess, and David took her hand in his own, very gently, and without a word he led her to the window. And as they stood there, hand in hand, the song of the little white bird was like sunshine, and the buds unfolded their silky petals till the tree was bright with golden yellow roses.

Then the princess knew that her dream had come true. She looked at the little white singing bird and loved it. And then she looked into David's eyes, and knew she would grow to love him too, more than bright yellow roses on a fresh young tree, more than a little white singing bird, more than anything else in the whole wide world.

I'm-the-One
and Not-Me

SKINNY LITTLE I'm-the-One and fat little Not-Me decided they would build a boat and sail it out to sea.

Then skinny little I'm-the-One said, "Which of us will build it?"

And fat little Not-Me said, "One of us. But not me."

So skinny little I'm-the-One said, "Very well then. I'm the one."

He sawed and he hammered and at last he made the *Caroline*, a single-masted sailing boat ready for the sea. Then he bought a compass, and some charts, and a log book. He stowed water cans and China tea and chocolate and oranges and pickled pork and nuts in the boat called the *Caroline*.

Then skinny little I'm-the-One said, "Which of us will sail her?"

And fat little Not-Me said, "One of us. But not me."

So skinny little I'm-the-One said, "Very well then. I'm the one."

He boarded the *Caroline* with fat little Not-Me, and hoisted sail, and away they went to sea. They sailed for seven hours beneath a bright blue sky. Then scudding little clouds appeared, then big heavy gray ones. A strong breeze blew, and the sea got choppy. The little boat called *Caroline* was tossed on the waves. Skinny little I'm-the-One reefed down the sail. But the sky grew darker and the sea grew rougher. A great surging wave lifted up the *Caroline*, and threw her in the air, and tipped her upside down.

Skinny little I'm-the-One and fat little Not-Me were tossed willy-nilly in the tumbling sea. The waves took them up, and carried them away, and washed them up safely on a faraway island.

The storm passed over and the sun came out. Skinny little I'm-the-One and fat little Not-Me were glad to be safe, but they both felt hungry. They decided they must live on mackerel and bananas.

Then skinny little I'm-the-One said, "Who's to catch the mackerel?"

And fat little Not-Me said, "One of us. But not me."

So skinny little I'm-the-One said, "Very well then. I'm the one."

First he made a fishing rod and caught some fine fat mackerel. After that he made a fire, and spiked the mackerel on a stick, and cooked them till they smelled delicious. Then skinny little I'm-the-One and fat little Not-Me ate up all the mackerel, which were very good indeed.

And then they decided they would like some bananas. There was just one banana tree growing on the island, and the sweet ripe bananas grew right at the top.

Then skinny little I'm-the-One said, "Which of us will pick them?"

And fat little Not-Me said, "One of us. But not me."

So skinny little I'm-the-One said, "Very well then. I'm the one."

He climbed up the tree, and it hurt his knees and elbows. But he picked the bananas and threw them down to Not-Me. Then skinny little I'm-the-One and fat little Not-Me ate the bananas, which were very good indeed.

By the end of a fortnight skinny little I'm-the-One and fat little Not-Me were very sad and homesick. They gazed out to sea, wanting to be rescued. But no boat came, and so they decided that the only thing to do was to make a little raft.

Then skinny little I'm-the-One said, "Which of us will make it?"

And fat little Not-Me said, "One of us. But not me."

So skinny little I'm-the-One said, "Very well then. I'm the one."

He made a raft of driftwood, with a stick for a mast, and he tied on his red woollen jersey for a sail. He got on the raft with fat little Not-Me, and they floated out gently on the flat blue sea. They looked all around them, still very homesick, hoping that a boat would come and take them off the raft.

Then a boat *did* come—a boat called *Tiny Tessa*. The sailor on the boat shouted, "Only room for one! She's a very small boat. I can only rescue one of you."

Then skinny little I'm-the-One said, "Which one will be rescued?"

And fat little Not-Me said, "One of us. And I'm the one."

So skinny little I'm-the-One said, "No you're not. I'm I'm-the-One."

So I'm-the-One was rescued, and he got on the boat, and before very long he was safe and sound at home.

Fat little Not-Me was left on the raft. He floated and he floated, and I *think* he got to Africa.

Puffalot

PUFFALOT WAS a branch line train. Every morning at 8:15 he left the station at Little Lacking and took his passengers into the town.

Every morning at ten past eight his passengers went to their favorite seats and sat there waiting for

Puffalot to start. From the platform you could see their heads at the windows.

There were:

Three noisy schoolboys in scarlet caps.

The Town Hall typist in a yellow silk scarf.

The gown shop lady in a gray fur beret.

The garage mechanic in a deerstalker hat.

The shoe shop assistant in a blue woollen hood.

And last of all, in a carriage by himself, the very important businessman, in a hard round bowler hat as black as a crow.

At 8:15 Puffalot started. He enjoyed his journey into the town, and all along the line he had friends to see. There was old Mr. Matchett at the level crossing, and young Ted Tubbins at the signal box. There were three little girls who waved from the bridge, and Mr. Pratt the porter at Hallingdon Halt. But Puffalot's favorite friend was a lady—the lady in the apron, halfway to town. She lived in the middle of a row of houses. They were red brick and sooty, with sheds at the back, and long straggly gardens with cabbages and clotheslines. The gardens came right to the railway line.

The lady in the apron was young and pretty, and nearly every morning she waved to Puffalot. The passengers thought she was waving to *them*, and all but one of them smiled and waved back. The lady in the apron could see them waving.

The three noisy schoolboys in scarlet caps.

The Town Hall typist in a yellow silk scarf.

The gown shop lady in a gray fur beret.

The garage mechanic in a deerstalker hat.

The shoe shop assistant in a blue woollen hood.

But last of all, in a carriage by himself, the very important businessman in a hard round bowler hat as black as a crow—*he* didn't wave. He was much too important.

All through the winter Puffalot was happy. In September the leaves fell down from the trees and old Mr. Matchett wore his brown woollen scarf. In October Ted Tubbins caught his usual cold. In November a thick gray fog crept up, and the lady in the apron was hidden behind it. In December there were paper chains and lights in all the windows, and the lady in the apron had a Christmas tree.

There was deep shining snow on the ground in January. Puffalot pushed harder to get along the line. It rained in February, day after day, and the three little girls wore their wellington boots. The freezing East winds blew strongly in March, and Mr. Pratt the porter had cold blue fingers. April came with sunshine, and the long straggly gardens had yellow clumps of daffodils growing here and there. The lady in the apron hung her washing on the line, and as Puffalot passed her she turned round to wave. And because it was springtime and the sun was shining, the passengers waved back more happily than usual.

Then, toward the end of April, a sad thing happened. As Puffalot came to the row of brick houses, the lady in the apron was nowhere to be seen. But there in the garden, on a small patch of grass, stood a smart new pram with a baby in it. Puffalot was so excited and happy that he whistled three times, and he wondered to himself if the baby would wave when he grew a little bigger.

But as Puffalot passed the little brick house, something happened that he couldn't understand. The baby screwed his eyes up and opened his mouth, and cried until his little face was pink and damp and angry. Then the lady in the apron ran from the house, and looked at Puffalot, but didn't wave.

All night long in the engine shed Puffalot wondered what he could do. He hadn't *meant* to frighten the baby. Perhaps little babies didn't like whistles. Puffalot felt better. He knew what to do.

Next morning, as he came to the row of brick houses, Puffalot closed his whistle up tight. The baby was there in the pram again, and Puffalot loved him.

He had bright blue eyes. Then Puffalot passed the little brick house with his whistle closed tight. He didn't whistle once.

But the baby screwed his eyes up, and opened his mouth, and cried until his little face was pink and damp and angry. Then the lady in the apron ran from the house, and she didn't wave to Puffalot. She frowned instead.

All night long in the engine shed, Puffalot stayed awake and worried. Perhaps little babies didn't like smoke. Puffalot decided what he would do.

Next morning, when he came to the row of brick houses, he puffed out his smoke in a special way. The baby was there, lying in the pram, and Puffalot loved him more than ever. He had one little tuft of fluffy hair curling from under his white woollen bonnet. Then Puffalot passed the little brick house, puffing his smoke to the other side.

But the baby screwed his eyes up and opened his mouth, and cried until his little face was pink and damp and angry. Then the lady in the apron ran from the house, and stared at Puffalot, cross and unfriendly.

All night long in the engine shed, Puffalot was worried and very unhappy. Perhaps little babies didn't like noise. Puffalot felt better. He knew what to do.

Next morning, as he came to the row of brick houses, he puffed very slowly along the line. The baby was there, more beautiful than ever. He had tiny fat hands, with dimples on them. Then Puffalot passed the little brick house very, very slowly indeed, puffing so softly there was hardly any sound.

But the baby screwed his eyes up, and opened his mouth, and cried until his little face was pink and damp and angry. Then the lady in the apron ran from the house, and called out something angrily to Puffalot.

Puffalot was too upset to hear her, and all through the night in the engine shed he worried and puzzled and grew more and more unhappy. He couldn't think of *anything* else that frightened little babies.

Next morning, as he came to the row of brick houses, the baby was there in the pram as usual, fat and contented and smiling at the sky. Then Puffalot knew that he couldn't go on. He just couldn't make the baby cry any more. So Puffalot puffed three more times, then he stopped.

For a minute or two the passengers were quiet, waiting for Puffalot to start again. Then they looked at their watches and wondered what was wrong.

"The signal's against us," said the three noisy schoolboys, and they opened the window and looked along the line. And the baby smiled at the three noisy schoolboys in their scarlet caps.

"It's a proper nuisance," said the Town Hall typist, and she opened the window and looked around her. And the baby smiled at the Town Hall typist in her yellow silk scarf.

"We shall all be late," said the gown shop lady, and she opened the window and put out her head. And the baby smiled at the gown shop lady in her gray fur beret.

"Must have broken down," said the garage mechanic, and he opened the window and shouted at the driver. And the baby smiled at the garage mechanic in his deerstalker hat.

"I'll be late again," said the shoe shop assistant, and she opened the window and waved at the schoolboys. And the baby smiled at the shoe shop assistant in her blue woollen hood.

Last of all, in a carriage by himself, the very important businessman looked at his watch and muttered to himself, "It's quite disgraceful. I shall make a complaint." Then he opened the window and put out his head.

The baby looked at the businessman in his hard

round bowler hat as black as a crow. And the baby screwed his eyes up, and opened his mouth, and cried until his little face was pink and damp and angry.

Then all the passengers turned their heads to look at the important businessman.

"It's his hat," said the schoolboys. "That's what it is. It's that hat that's making the baby cry."

"And I'm not surprised," said the Town Hall typist. "It's black as a crow and twice as ugly."

"He should really take it off," said the gown shop lady.

"Take it off, Mister," said the garage mechanic.

"To please the little baby," said the shoe shop assistant.

The very important businessman looked at the baby and the baby's mother. Then he looked at the passengers, and took off his hat.

The baby hiccupped, and opened his eyes. The very important businessman and the pink-faced baby stared at each other. Then the very important businessman saw the baby's blue eyes, and his tuft of hair, and his fat little hands with the dimples on them. And the very important businessman smiled at the baby, and the baby smiled back. Then the baby chuckled, and hiccupped again, and the lady in the apron started to laugh.

Then the schoolboys laughed, and the Town Hall

typist, and the gown shop lady, and the garage mechanic and the shoe shop assistant laughed. And last of all, in a carriage by himself, the very important businessman suddenly laughed for the first time in years.

Puffalot sighed a long, happy sigh. Then he got up steam, and whistled three times, and puffed along the line past the little brick house. And the baby chuckled and bounced in his pram, and beat his fat little hands in the air.

"He's waving," thought Puffalot. "He likes me. He's waving."

And because he was suddenly happy again, Puffalot puffed more quickly than usual. So no one was late for work, after all.

Grandmother Gregory

GRANDMOTHER GREGORY sat by the fireside, and sighed to herself. She was all alone. On this autumn evening she had no one to talk to, and no one was sitting in the big brown chair on the other side of the leaping fire.

"What a pity!" Grandmother Gregory said. "I

wish that a nice old gentleman was there. He'd be someone to talk to, and share the fire. But what's the use of wishing? I'll save my breath. My wishes don't come true any more."

Long years ago they *had* come true. When her hair had been soft and black as night, and her eyes as bright as twinkling stars, she had known how to conjure up magic spells. They had called her a witch, and perhaps she was, but now she was old and her spells were forgotten.

"All forgotten!" said Grandmother Gregory. "But perhaps if I searched at the back of my mind I could *try* to remember. It could do no harm. Now, let me see. What do I say? Hocus-pocus, that's the beginning."

Grandmother Gregory closed her eyes. "Hocus-pocus," she said to herself. "Hocus-pocus, and what comes next?

Hocus-pocus, sixty-two,
Make my wish come quick and true.
Someone sitting on the chair
By the fireside over there."

Grandmother Gregory opened her eyes and looked across at the big brown chair. And there, curled up on the red velvet cushion, was a fat black cat.

"Fancy that!" said Grandmother Gregory. "*You're* not a nice old gentleman, are you? But now I come to think of it, a fat black cat is just the right person to sit by the fireside."

Next morning Grandmother Gregory gave the fat black cat a saucer of milk and a little bit of fish, and then she let him out into the orchard. There were windfalls beneath the apple tree.

"Such a lot of apples," said Grandmother Gregory. "Far too many for *me* to eat. What a pity there isn't a nice old gentleman to help me eat all these fine red apples."

Grandmother Gregory closed her eyes. "Hocus-pocus," she said to herself.

> "Hocus-pocus, sixty-two,
> Make my wish come quick and true.
> Someone I should like to see
> Underneath my apple tree."

Grandmother Gregory opened her eyes, and there beneath the apple tree was a little pink pig, chumping up the apples.

"Goodness me!" said Grandmother Gregory. "You don't look at all like a nice old gentleman. But now I come to think of it, a little pink pig is just the right person for eating up apples."

Next morning Grandmother Gregory gave the black cat a saucer of milk and a little bit of fish, and then she let him out into the orchard. The little pink pig had rolled in the mud, so she washed him all over with warm soapy water.

The grass in the orchard had grown so tall that it almost hid the little pink pig.

"What a pity!" Grandmother Gregory said. "It has grown so long that it's almost hay. I wish that a nice old gentleman was here, to crop the grass and keep it short."

Grandmother Gregory closed her eyes. "Hocus-pocus," she said to herself.

> "Hocus-pocus, sixty-two,
> Make my wish come quick and true.
> Someone here this very day
> To crop the grass before it's hay."

Grandmother Gregory opened her eyes. And there in the orchard was a plump red cow cropping the grass.

"Would you believe it!" said Grandmother Gregory. "You're not in the least like a nice old gentleman. But all the same, now I come to think of it, a plump red cow is just the right person to crop the grass and keep it short."

Next morning Grandmother Gregory gave the

black cat a saucer of milk and a little bit of fish, and let him out into the orchard. Then she washed the little pink pig. And then she milked the plump red cow.

"It's fine creamy milk," she said to herself. "I shall make a rice pudding."

Grandmother Gregory made the rice pudding and put it into the oven to cook. And she roasted a leg of lamb as well, so as not to waste the heat of the oven. When dinner time came she ate all the pudding, but she couldn't finish the leg of lamb.

"I'm full right up," she said to herself. "But there's still some good roast lamb on the plate. What a pity it has to be left to get cold. I wish that a nice old gentleman was here, to eat up the leftovers."

Grandmother Gregory closed her eyes. "Hocus-pocus," she said to herself.

"Hocus-pocus, sixty-two,
Make my wish come quick and true.
Someone coming through the door
To clear the plate and ask for more."

Grandmother Gregory opened her eyes, and in through the door came a little brown dog. He ate up the rest of the good roast lamb and buried the bone in a corner of the garden.

"Mercy me!" said Grandmother Gregory. "That's the strangest old gentleman I ever saw! But now I come to think of it a little brown dog is just the right person for eating leftovers."

Next morning Grandmother Gregory gave the black cat a saucer of milk and a little bit of fish, and let him out into the orchard. Then she washed the little pink pig. Then she milked the plump red cow. And then she took the little brown dog for a walk in the park. Grandmother Gregory looked at the flowers; she fed the ducks in the pond; she talked to the mothers with babies in prams, and cooed at the babies until they chuckled. That evening she sat alone by the fireside, remembering the things she had seen in the park.

"So many things!" she said to herself. "Enough to make a story. I dearly love stories. What a pity there isn't a nice old gentleman to sit by the fireside and listen while I tell them."

Grandmother Gregory closed her eyes. "Hocus-pocus," she said to herself.

"Hocus-pocus, sixty-two,
Make my wish come quick and true.
Someone who will never tire
Of stories told beside the fire."

Grandmother Gregory opened her eyes. And there on the big brown chair was a boy. The fat black cat

was lying on his lap, and the little brown dog was sitting at his feet.

"Well I never!" said Grandmother Gregory. "A nice old gentleman, so that's what you are! But now I come to think of it, a little boy is just the right person for listening to stories."

Grandmother Gregory told her story, all about the park, and the ducks, and the babies. The little boy listened, and sometimes he smiled. The black cat purred, and the dog wagged his tail.

"And that's the end," said Grandmother Gregory. "It's long past your bedtime."

The little boy yawned, and he yawned again as Grandmother Gregory tucked him into bed. Then he said, "You'll be all by yourself now, won't you? What a pity there isn't a nice old gentleman."

Grandmother Gregory threw up her hands.

"A nice old gentleman indeed!" she said. "And how would I find the time for *him?* Do you know what I do every day of my life? I give the black cat a saucer of milk and a little bit of fish and I let him out into the orchard. Then I wash the little pink pig. Then I milk the plump red cow. Then I take the little brown dog for a walk in the park. And then I tell you stories. I'm far too busy for a nice old gentleman."

Then Grandmother Gregory went downstairs and smiled to herself as she sat by the fireside.

The Five
Little Men

ONCE UPON A TIME there were five little men called Thomas, Timothy, Titus, Tobias and Tod.

They all lived together in a little brick house with a green front door and a red-tiled roof. And they all looked alike.

Each little man had a cheerful round face.

Each little man had nut-brown hair.

Each little man was tubby round the middle.

And they all had birthdays on the fifth of December.

So each little man was exactly like the next one, and no one could tell the difference between them.

"We all look exactly alike, of course," said the five little men. "But it doesn't matter."

Then early one morning when the sun was shining the five little men met five little ladies. The five little ladies were not at all alike, except that each of them was thin as a wafer, and each of them chirruped like a bird when she spoke.

Thomas, Timothy, Titus, Tobias and Tod married the five little chirruping ladies, and they all lived together in the little brick house.

"They all look exactly alike, of course," said the five little ladies. "But it doesn't matter."

But on Monday morning at breakfast time they found it *did* matter.

Mrs. Thomas cooked porridge for Thomas and gave it to Timothy.

Mrs. Timothy cooked eggs for Timothy and gave them to Titus.

Mrs. Titus cooked haddock for Titus and gave it to Tobias.

Mrs. Tobias cooked ham for Tobias and gave it to Tod.

Mrs. Tod cooked kippers for Tod and gave them to Thomas.

Then the five little men sat round the breakfast table, pulling faces, and saying to each other, "That's *my* breakfast. You've got *my* breakfast."

"We're very sorry," said the five little ladies. "But how can we tell the difference between you?"

Then the five little ladies went to the parlor and sat in a row on the yellow velvet sofa. They talked together and made a plan. Then they went back to the five little men.

"You all look exactly alike," they said. "And it *does* matter.

"You must each of you go out into the world— North, South, East and West.

"Then you will see that people look different.

"And when you come back, *you* must look different.

"And you mustn't come back till the fifth of December, and then we will give you a birthday party."

The five little men grizzled and grumbled. Then all of them packed their ditty bags, with pajamas and a toothbrush and a clean pair of socks. And all of them set out into the world.

At the end of the road they parted company, each of them going his separate way.

Thomas went North.

After seven days he came to a seaport, where the great gray ships lay quiet and still, waiting to sail the seven seas. On the deck of one of them a sea captain stood, seven feet tall and strong as an oak. And his fine bushy beard was as red as the sunrise.

Thomas smiled to himself, and said, "That's what I'll do. I'll grow a beard. Then I'll look different from all the others."

So that was that.

Timothy went South.

After seven days he came to a place where little pink houses stood close to a lake. The lake was wide and still and blue and the air was soft and warm with sunshine. In the garden of one of the little pink houses an artist was painting a pink and gold picture. His eyes were as quiet and blue as the lake. And his little pointed beard was as brown as a nut.

Timothy smiled to himself, and said, "That's what I'll do. I'll grow a beard. Then I'll look different from all the others."

So that was that.

Titus went East.

After seven days he came to a place where camels traveled over hot sandy deserts to seven tall palm trees beside a well. In the shade of one of the trees sat a fortuneteller, drawing mysterious signs in the sand. His hands were as brown as mahogany wood, and his long flowing beard was as black as a crow.

Titus smiled to himself, and said, "That's what I'll do. I'll grow a beard. Then I'll look different from all the others."

So that was that.

Tobias went West.

After seven days he came to a city full of great old buildings and wide green rivers. In one of the buildings sat grave-faced students, and in front of them all sat a wise old professor, speaking wise old words. The professor was as thin as a bean pole, and his long straggly beard was as gray as slate.

Tobias smiled to himself, and said, "That's what I'll do. I'll grow a beard. Then I'll look different from all the others."

So that was that.

There was nowhere left for Tod to go. So he sat on top of a five-barred gate and talked to the billy goat who lived in the field. The billy goat only said, "Baa! Baa!" and waggled his little white beard at Tod.

Tod said, "Bah! You funny old billy goat. That's

what I'll do. I'll grow a beard. Then I'll look different from all the others.

So that was that.

Back at home in the little brick house the five little ladies waited and waited, until it came to the fifth of December. Then they bustled about with their aprons on, making a cake for the birthday party.

"They'll be here very soon," said the five little ladies. "They'll soon be here—our five little men.

"And they'll all look different.

"Quite, quite different.

"Five times different, our five little men."

Then the five little ladies set the table, and iced the cake, and got out the candles. And as they put the fifth red candle on the cake, the doorbell rang.

"They're here!" cried the five little ladies. "They're here!" And they ran from the kitchen to open the door.

There on the doorstep stood the five little men.

Each little man had a cheerful round face.

Each little man had nut-brown hair.

Each little man was tubby round the middle.

And each little man had a nut-brown beard.

"Oh no, no, no!" cried the five little ladies,

and they threw their aprons over their heads.

Then the five little ladies recovered themselves. While the five little men sat in the kitchen, the five little ladies went to the parlor. They took out their knitting bags and sat on the sofa. And they knitted, click-clack, and knitted, clack-click. Then they wrapped their knitting in five little parcels, in birthday paper. They addressed the parcels to Thomas, Timothy, Titus, Tobias and Tod, and put one on each of the little men's plates on the parlor table.

"Now," they said. "It's time for tea."

Then the five little men and the five little ladies had a birthday party.

"Open your presents," said the five little ladies. "Look, there are five little parcels on your plates."

The five little men opened their parcels, and out came five little knitted round hats. Thomas, Timothy, Titus, Tobias and Tod were delighted.

"We shall wear them forever and ever," they said.

So there they sat, the five little men, in their five little hats.

Thomas had a blue one.

Timothy had a green one.

Titus had an orange one.

Tobias had a yellow one.

Tod had a red one.

So each little man looked different from the next one, and *anyone* could tell the difference between them. And from that day forward they *always* looked different, because they were so delighted with their hats that they never took them off. They wore them all the time.

They wore them at breakfast time and dinner time and supper time.

They wore them for chopping wood, and washing up, and gardening.

They wore them in the bath.

They wore them in bed.

The five little ladies chirruped like birds, and the five little men whistled a tune. And they all lived happily ever after.

The Day the Postman Came to Tea

THERESA LOOKED out of the window, and it was still raining. She breathed on the windowpane until it was misty, and then she drew a fat round cat with her finger. It had six little whiskers and a long curly tail.

"Don't do that," said Theresa's mother. "It makes

the glass smeary. Why don't you draw in your drawing book?"

"I've *done* that," Theresa said. "I've done everything."

Theresa's mother looked out of the window. It was still raining.

"Put on your raincoat and your wellington boots. You can go to the village and do some shopping. You'd better take an umbrella with you. Mine's no use, it lets in the rain. So you'd better take Daddy's. But mind you don't lose it."

When Theresa was ready, her mother said, "Here's a ten shilling note. Get a large tube of toothpaste from Baxter the Chemist, half a pound of toffees from old Mrs. Mason, a small tin of cat food for Tibs from the pet shop, post this letter to Auntie Peggy, and don't lose Daddy's best umbrella. Can you remember all that?"

"I think I can," Theresa said.

She tucked the letter into her pocket, and picked up the shopping bag. Then she walked along the road beneath the umbrella, like a big black mushroom with legs.

Squish, squish, squish went her wellington boots. A large tube of toothpaste from Baxter the Chemist, half a pound of toffees from old Mrs. Mason, a small tin of cat food for Tibs from the pet shop, post the letter to Auntie Peggy, and don't lose Daddy's best umbrella.

Baxter the Chemist's shop window was full of cough mixtures and cold cures. Theresa put down the big black umbrella and hung the crook carefully over her arm. Then she went in.

"A large tube of Abasent Toothpaste, please."

"That's three and eleven," said Mr. Baxter. "Anything else you're needing today?"

"No, thank you, that's all," Theresa told him.

Outside the shop, she put up the umbrella and went a little farther along the road.

Squish, squish, squish went her wellington boots. Half a pound of toffees from old Mrs. Mason, a small tin of cat food for Tibs from the pet shop, post the letter to Auntie Peggy, and don't lose Daddy's best umbrella.

Old Mrs. Mason's shop window was full of bars of chocolate and Assorted Mixtures. Theresa put down the big black umbrella and hung the crook carefully over her arm. Then she went in.

"Half a pound of Comfits Creamy Toffees, please."

"That's one and eightpence," said old Mrs. Mason. "Not wanting licorice allsorts today?"

"Not today, thank you," Theresa told her.

Outside the shop, she put up the umbrella and went a little farther along the road.

Squish, squish, squish went her wellington boots. A small tin of cat food for Tibs from the pet shop, post the letter to Auntie Peggy, and don't lose Daddy's best umbrella.

The pet shop window was full of rubber bones and birdcages, and packages of fish food. Theresa put down the big black umbrella and hung the crook carefully over her arm. Then she went in.

"A small tin of Kittipurr cat food please."

"Tenpence please," said the man behind the counter. "Is it still raining cats and dogs outside?"

"Yes, but I've got an umbrella," said Theresa.

Outside the shop, she put up the umbrella and went a little farther along the road.

Squish, squish, squish went her wellington boots. Post the letter to Auntie Peggy and don't lose Daddy's best umbrella.

The post office clock said twenty to four.

"Nearly tea time," Theresa thought.

"Just in time," said a voice she knew. "It's lucky for you I'm ten minutes late."

"Hello, postman," Theresa said. "I suppose you've come to collect the letters."

"That's the idea," the postman said. "So if you're

going to post one, pop it in quickly. Not lost it, have you?"

"No," said Theresa. "It's somewhere in my pocket. But I haven't got a hand left to find it."

She put down the umbrella and propped it against the post office wall. Then she put the shopping bag beside it, and searched in both her pockets for the letter.

"Got it?" said the postman. "Good! Pop it in. And don't you forget your father's umbrella."

"He'd be very cross if I did," said Theresa.

She put up the umbrella and set off for home, like a big black mushroom with legs. *Squish, squish, squish,* went her wellington boots. Don't lose Daddy's best umbrella. Don't lose Daddy's best umbrella.

"Well I haven't lost it, so there," thought Theresa.

In the kitchen at home, tea was nearly ready.

"Oh good," said Theresa. "Chocolate swiss roll! Look, Mummy, I didn't lose it. I *didn't* lose Daddy's best umbrella."

"Good," said her mother. "Well done, Theresa." And she and Theresa smiled at each other. "Give me the tin of cat food, dear. Tibs wants his tea."

Suddenly both their faces were solemn.

"Oh goodness me!" said Theresa's mother. "You

remembered Daddy's best umbrella, and forgot the shopping."

Theresa stared down at her empty hands.

"Try to remember," her mother said. "Where did you leave it?"

"It wasn't at the chemist's," said Theresa. "And it wasn't at old Mrs. Mason's either. And it wasn't at the pet shop, I had it then. And after that I went to. . . . Oh Mummy, it's out in the rain, it's outside the. . . ."

Then the doorbell rang. Theresa's mother opened the door, and a post office van was parked at the curbside. The postman stood on the doorstep, smiling, and holding something behind his back.

"The mail?" Theresa's mother was puzzled. "At this time of day?"

"Special delivery," the postman said. "No extra charge!" And he held out the shopping bag.

"So that's where she left it," said Theresa's mother. "Outside the post office. Thank you, postman. Thank you very much. Have you got time for a cup of tea?"

"Always got time for tea," said the postman, and he followed Theresa's mother to the kitchen.

"And there's chocolate swiss roll," Theresa told him.

"Good!" said the postman. "My favorite food!"
And he ate three slices.

Old Mrs. Middling

OLD MRS. WATT lived at Number Eleven, in the middle of a neat little row of houses. Each of the houses had a garden in front, a small, square garden with a low brick wall. *Most* of the gardens were neat and tidy, with smooth green lawns, and trim little borders, full of tulips in the springtime and petunias in the summer.

But Number Eleven's garden was different. The little square lawn was rough and tangled, and the border was full of groundsel weeds.

On Saturday afternoons in the summer, *most* people got their lawn mowers out, and mowed their lawns, and trimmed the edges. And then they hoed between the petunias.

But no one came out of Number Eleven. Old Mrs. Watt was a sad old lady, and from Monday to Saturday nobody saw her, and she saw nobody, except one person—a different person every day.

On Monday the postman called; on Tuesday, the grocer; on Wednesday, the laundryman; on Thursday, the dustman; on Friday, the butcher came; on Saturday, the milkman. On Sunday, nobody called at all.

Every Monday, round about breakfast time, the postman brought a letter in a square blue envelope. It came from old Mrs. Watt's married sister, who lived in the village a mile or so away.

"Morning, Ma'am," said the postman. "Nice morning! And how are you keeping? Well, I hope."

"Middling," said old Mrs. Watt. "Fair to middling. 'Tis the twinges in my joints."

On Tuesday the grocer came in his van, with tea and sugar and best dairy butter, and eggs and bacon and washing powder, and matches and marmalade and wheatmeal biscuits—and anything else Mrs. Watt might fancy.

"Morning," he said. "Eggs today? Keeping well?"

"Middling," said old Mrs. Watt. "Fair to middling. 'Tis the wheezes in my chest."

On Wednesday the laundryman knocked at the door, with a big blue box full of clean white washing.

"Going to be a nice fine day," he said. "And how are you keeping? Not too bad, I hope."

"Middling," said old Mrs. Watt. "Fair to middling. 'Tis my poor old aching feet."

On Thursday the dustman called for the rubbish.

"Morning," he said. "Keeping well as usual?"

"Middling," said old Mrs. Watt. "Fair to middling. 'Tis the twitching in my fingers."

On Friday the butcher brought the weekend joint, and some good beef suet, and half a pound of sausages.

"Morning. Nice bit of brisket," he said. "Colder today. And how are you keeping?"

"Middling," said old Mrs. Watt. "Fair to middling. 'Tis the dimness in my eyes."

On Saturday the milkman came to the door.

"Six and fivepence halfpenny this week," he said. "Not bad weather, considering, is it?"

"Middling," said old Mrs. Watt. "Fair to middling. 'Tis a hard life."

On Sunday nobody called at all. Old Mrs. Watt's married sister often said, "Why don't you come and visit us on Sundays?" But old Mrs. Watt said it couldn't be managed.

"I'm better to stay at home," she said. " 'Tis the twinges in my joints, and the wheezes in my chest, and my poor old aching feet, and the twitching in my fingers, and the dimness in my eyes. 'Tis a hard life."

Hard it was, for old Mrs. Watt. Spring came at last, and early summer. But even in the sunshine she felt no better.

"I'm middling," she would say. "Just fair to middling." So that after a time no one called her Mrs. Watt. They called her Mrs. Middling, poor old Mrs. Middling.

And then something happened that made a difference. Poor old Mrs. Middling heard it from the postman.

"Going to be a bus along this road," he said. "The 206. Changing the route."

"A bus?" said Mrs. Middling. "Who wants a bus?

We've managed without one for the last twenty years. What do we want with them noisy old things?"

"Useful for getting to the village," said the postman.

But old Mrs. Middling said, "Nasty noisy things! And them horrid smelly gasoline fumes is wicked on my chest."

On Thursday the dustman said, "Looks like you're lucky. Having the bus stop so near! Nice and handy."

Old Mrs. Middling muttered to herself as she watched the workmen putting up the sign. BUS STOP it said, in red and white.

"Right outside my own front door," said Mrs. Middling. "I don't know how I'll stand it. I really don't."

On Saturday the buses came along the road. Mrs. Middling watched them from behind her curtains. Every time a bus stopped, some people got off. Then *ping!* went the bell, and on went the bus.

"I'll *never* get used to it," said old Mrs. Middling.

By Saturday tea time things were worse than ever. There were six little crumpled bits of paper on her lawn.

"Throwing down their tickets!" said old Mrs. Middling. "Too bone idle to put them in the box."

By Sunday tea time the little front lawn had tickets all over it, and old Mrs. Middling watched from her window and grumbled to herself. "Disgraceful it is. And who's to pick them up? I'll have to do it myself, I suppose. And me with these terrible twinges in my joints."

On Monday morning old Mrs. Middling went out into her little front garden and started to pick up the tickets from the lawn. Her old bones creaked as she stooped, and groaned, and heaved herself up again, and groaned again, and grumbled. But she went on working, and after an hour, she had picked up all the tickets from the little front lawn.

Then old Mrs. Middling went indoors, and put on the kettle for a cup of tea. And as she reached up to the shelf for the tea caddy: "Mercy me!" she said to herself. "The twinges in my joints have gone right away."

On Tuesday morning old Mrs. Middling saw six more tickets on her little front lawn. She went outside to pick them up, and as she worked she grumbled to herself: "They get tangled in this long old grass, that's the nuisance. I could pick them up better if the lawn was mowed. And who's to do it? Myself, I suppose, and me with these terrible wheezes in my chest."

Old Mrs. Middling went to the shed and got out the mower. It was rusty and it squeaked. She found the oil can and oiled out the squeaks, and then she started to mow the lawn. She puffed and she wheezed and she pushed and she pulled and she groaned and she grumbled, but she went on working. By the end of the morning the lawn was short and smooth.

Old Mrs. Middling put the mower away, and went to the bathroom to wash her hands. And as she climbed the stairs: "Mercy me!" she said. "The wheezes in my chest have all gone away."

On Wednesday morning there were only three tickets on old Mrs. Middling's neat little lawn. "My!" she said. "That lawn looks handsome. But it shows up the weeds in the border quite nasty."

So old Mrs. Middling pulled up the groundsel weeds and threw them away on the rubbish heap. The border looked bare with nothing in it.

"It's needing some plants," said Old Mrs. Middling. "And who's to go and get them? Myself, I suppose. And me with my poor old aching feet."

Old Mrs. Middling put on her coat, and set off down the road on her way to the village. She plodded and she grumbled and she hobbled and she muttered, but she went on walking to the gardening shop. Then back she came, still grumbling and hobbling, with three dozen little petunia plants. She put them carefully into a bucket, with water at the bottom to keep them fresh.

Then old Mrs. Middling put on the kettle, and went to the cupboard for her comfy old slippers. And as she put them on: "Mercy me!" she said. "The aches in my feet have gone right away."

On Thursday morning there were only two tickets on old Mrs. Middling's neat little lawn. She looked at the little petunia plants. They were starting to droop in spite of the water.

"Ought to be put in the border," she said. "And who's to do it? Myself, I suppose. And me with my poor old twitching fingers."

Old Mrs. Middling got a trowel from the shed, and she planted the little petunia seedlings. She patted and smoothed the earth around them, so that the roots were held firmly in the soil. And as she worked, she grumbled and groaned, but she went on digging little holes with her trowel, and planting the seedlings, and patting down the soil. It was almost dinner time before she had finished. Then she went to the kitchen to cook some eggs and bacon. And as she cut the rinds from the bacon: "Mercy! The twitching in my fingers has gone right away," she said.

On Friday morning there was only one ticket in old Mrs. Middling's neat little garden. She got the watering can from the shed and watered the little petunia plants. And as she worked she grumbled a little, but she went on watering the strong little seedlings. Then a boy came and sat on the little brick wall in front of old Mrs. Middling's garden. He was looking at a book as he waited for the bus, but he sighed rather sadly as he looked at the pictures.

"The bus won't be long," said old Mrs. Middling. "Read yourself a story, dear, and pass away the time."

"I can't," said the boy. "Because I can't read."

"Oh, dear me!" said old Mrs. Middling. "Then who's to read it? Myself, I suppose. And me with this nasty old dimness in my eyes."

Old Mrs. Middling fetched her reading glasses, and sat on the little brick wall beside the boy. She read a funny story, and the little boy laughed. The bus came along when the story finished, and the little boy waved as he ran to catch it.

"That bus was shocking late," said old Mrs. Middling, and she went indoors to look at the clock. And as she looked: "Mercy me!" she said. "The dimness in my eyes has gone right away."

On Saturday morning there was not a single ticket in old Mrs. Middling's little front garden. It was such

a tidy, well cared for little garden that no one would have dreamed of spoiling it with tickets. Old Mrs. Middling looked from her window and saw that the sun was shining quite brightly. So she took her old basket chair out of the kitchen and put it in the middle of the neat little lawn. Then she sat on the chair in her own front garden, smiling to herself and enjoying the sunshine.

Every time a bus came, some people got off. They smiled at Mrs. Middling. "Nice morning," they said. Or "Isn't it lovely?" Or "Going to be hot." And old Mrs. Middling nodded and smiled. Once, an old gentleman got off the bus. "What a charming garden you have," he said. "Surely you don't do it all by yourself?" Then old Mrs. Middling nodded proudly, and they talked about gardens, and other things. "It's nice to have a friend," thought old Mrs. Middling.

The bus conductors were friendly, too. "Enjoying the sunshine? That's the way," they called. Then the boy who couldn't read came along with his book, and he leaned on the arm of the basket chair while old Mrs. Middling read him a story.

And old Mrs. Middling felt as happy as a lark. At the end of the day, when the sun went down: "Mercy! 'Tis a good old life," she said.

On Sunday morning old Mrs. Middling put on her best silk dress, and her hat, and her navy blue coat, and her white cotton gloves. Then she locked the back door and stood by the bus stop. She was going to visit her married sister.

"I could walk, really," said old Mrs. Middling. "But I rather fancy a bit of a ride. Handy, having the bus stop so near." Then the bus came along. Mrs. Middling got on. "A four-penny please," she told the conductor. *Ping!* went the bell, and off they went.

Old Mrs. Middling's married sister was quite astonished.

" 'Tis a miracle," she said. " 'Tis years since I've seen you so bright and well."

Old Mrs. Middling chuckled to herself.

"It weren't no miracle at all," she said. " 'Twere the buses what did it, and them nasty little tickets."

The Queen
Who Wore Pink

⁓ ONCE UPON A TIME in a faraway country there lived a queen who always wore pink.

"It's a beautiful color," she said to the King. "I shall always wear pink forever and ever."

And sure enough, all her clothes were pink, even her shoes and her gloves and her hats.

There *had* been a time when the King liked pink, too. But now he was tired of it, very tired. He was so tired of pink that he said to the Queen, "Your eyes are a beautiful blue, my dear. Blue would suit you, I'm sure it would."

"Pink!" said the Queen. "I prefer to wear pink."

"Green is pleasant," said the King. "Very pleasant. The color of trees and grass. It would suit you."

"Pink!" said the Queen. "It's the very best color."

The King sighed, and went away, wondering what he could do about it. How could he ever persuade the Queen to wear anything else but pink?

Then the Queen went away to visit her daughter. And as soon as she had gone the King became busy. The palace was suddenly full of workmen. They were painting the walls, and stitching curtains, and putting down carpets as fast as they could. By the end of the week they had finished their work, and the King looked around and was very pleased. Everything was bright, fresh pink. The walls were pink, the curtains were pink, the carpets were pink, and the chairs were pink. Even the lampshades and vases were pink.

"And today the Queen will come back," said the King, and he went to meet her at the palace front door.

"I'm sure you'll be pleased, my dear," he said.

"While you were away I had workmen in. They painted the walls, and they hung up new curtains, and they put down new carpets. It's all very smart."

The Queen went eagerly into the palace.

"Pink!" she cried. "It's delightful, my dear."

But after two days she wasn't so sure. The servant maids appeared wearing bright pink dresses, and the Queen rubbed her eyes and complained of a headache.

After two more days her headache was worse. At dinner time the tablecloth was pink—and the plates. The maid served pink salmon, then pink blancmange. The Queen complained of spots in front of her eyes.

"Just indigestion, my dear," said the King.

And the Queen wailed, "It's dreadful, because they're *pink* spots."

So the Queen went upstairs to lie down for an hour. But the sheets and blankets on her bed were pink, and when she fell asleep she had a bad pink dream. She dreamed that she turned bright pink all over. Even her eyes and her hair were pink.

Then the Queen woke up and screamed for the King.

"Whatever is the matter, my love?" said the King.

"It's pink, pink, pink, that's the matter," wailed the Queen. "It's a horrible color. Pink, pink, pink! I never want to see anymore of it—ever."

"Just as you say, my dear," said the King.

Next day, the palace was full of workmen. They were painting the walls, and stitching curtains, and putting down carpets as fast as they could. By the end of the day the walls were painted white, the curtains were blue, and the carpets were gold. The King called the Queen.

"Come and look, my dear," he said.

"I can't," wailed the Queen. "I've nothing to wear. All the dresses that I have are that horrible pink."

Then four little messenger boys appeared, bringing four big boxes, which they took to the Queen.

"Open them, my dear," said the King to the Queen.

The Queen took the lids off the big white boxes, and took out the dresses that were folded inside.

"Blue!" she cried. "It matches my eyes. And green —it's beautiful! And what a lovely yellow! And this pale gray silk is exactly what I wanted."

The King went away and counted his money.

"It cost me a fortune," he said to himself. "But the Queen will never wear pink again."

And she didn't!

The Galloping Hedgehog

HEDGEHOG LIVED IN a vegetable garden, with his hedgehog wife and his three hedgehog cousins.

He spent much of his time among the cabbages and lettuces, looking for fat gray slugs to eat. Whenever he wanted someone to talk to, there was always his wife or one of his cousins. If he wanted to look at the outside world, he went to the fence and looked through a hole.

The fence was very long. It stood straight and tall, all down one side of the vegetable garden. Close to the ground, spaced along this fence, were five little holes.

"And they're just the right size to be useful," said Hedgehog. "Too small to let dogs in—the nasty things—but big enough for looking through and seeing the world."

"The world" was a pavement, and as Hedgehog watched, his snout and two eyes just fitting the hole, he saw legs passing by. There were legs in trousers, and legs in stockings, and fat little trotting legs in socks. The world was an interesting place, thought Hedgehog.

And then one morning as he watched the world through the largest of the five little holes in the fence, Hedgehog had a sudden and disturbing shock. Two black eyes were staring at him from a hairy brown face that was close to his own.

Hedgehog drew back, and the hairy creature snuffled, "I suppose you think you're safe—behind that fence."

"Well, I am," said Hedgehog. "And who are you, coming and disturbing a peaceful hedgehog?"

"I'm Slobbery Dog," said the hairy creature. "And I'll jump right over the fence. And I'll get you."

"You couldn't," said Hedgehog. "The fence is too high. And even if you did, I should run away."

Slobbery Dog sat on his haunches, and lifted his head, and howled with laughter.

"Run?" he said, when he'd finished laughing. "You can only scuttle trot. You can't *run*."

Hedgehog was a peaceable, even-tempered creature, but he hated being laughed at by Slobbery Dog.

"Oh! Can't I?" he said. "Well, I'm telling you something. I could race you, and win. I'm the Galloping Hedgehog."

Slobbery Dog sat on his haunches, and laughed so much that he couldn't speak.

"What's more," said Hedgehog, "I'll prove it to you. You can run up and down on *your* side of the fence, and I'll gallop up and down on *my* side of the fence. And you'll see, I'll race you, Slobbery Dog."

Slobbery Dog said, "When shall we start?"

"Before I gallop, I sleep," said Hedgehog. "I have forty winks to get up my strength. So that's what I'll do, and then I'll come back."

Slobbery Dog went on laughing, and Hedgehog scuttled away from the fence, and disappeared from sight among the cabbages and lettuces.

But Hedgehog didn't have forty winks. He went to find his wife and his three hedgehog cousins. And when he had found them he told them what to do. Then back he went to the fence, scuttle trot, and he put his little snout through the first of the holes.

His hedgehog wife went, scuttle trot, to the second hole in the fence.

His first cousin went, scuttle trot, to the third hole in the fence.

His second cousin went, scuttle trot, to the fourth hole in the fence.

His third cousin went, scuttle trot, to the last hole in the fence.

So behind each hole in the fence was a hedgehog. They didn't show their snouts. They just sat there, waiting.

Then Hedgehog called through *his* hole in the fence, "Slobbery Dog, are you ready to race?"

Slobbery Dog said, "Wow-wow-wow. Of course I'm ready. One, two, three, go!"

Then Slobbery Dog went racing away, calling, "Wow-wow-wow, silly galloping hedgehog. I'll have run to the end of this old fence before you've had time to think about starting."

But when Slobbery Dog got to the second hole in the fence, a little hedgehog snout appeared, and a hedgehog voice called, "Look, I'm here. I'm here before you, Slobbery Dog."

Slobbery Dog was very surprised. He went on running, faster than ever. But when he got to the third hole, a little hedgehog snout appeared, and a hedgehog voice called, "What did I tell you? You'll have to run faster, Slobbery Dog."

Slobbery Dog ran faster still, but when he got to the fourth hole, a little hedgehog snout appeared, and a hedgehog voice called, "Poor old dog. Why don't you gallop, Slobbery Dog?"

Slobbery Dog raced like the wind, but when he got to the last hole, a little hedgehog snout appeared, and a hedgehog voice called, "Goodness me! You're dreadfully slow. I've been waiting for you."

Slobbery Dog howled with rage. Then he turned round, and ran back along the fence, faster than he'd ever run in his life. But every time he got to a hole, a little hedgehog snout appeared, and a hedgehog voice called, "Faster, faster! Can't you keep up with me, Slobbery Dog?"

Slobbery Dog ran up and down, up and down, all afternoon and evening. And at last he ran away, with his tail between his legs. As the stars came out, he sat on his haunches, and howled and howled at the bright new moon.

Then the five little hedgehogs in the vegetable garden said: "*He* won't bother us again, that's certain." And off they went to their supper, scuttle trot.

A Sailor for Kate

ONCE UPON A TIME there were four sisters, called Eleanor, Rosamund, Sarah and Kate.

Eleanor, the eldest, was tall and proud, with long golden hair that swung to her waist. She spent most of her time in front of her mirror, brushing her hair until it gleamed like fire. And when she looked up from her mirror she said, "On my seventeenth birthday I shall marry a prince. And my wedding gown will be shining silver."

Rosamund's eyes were as blue as the lake, and full of dreams. And when she woke from her dreams she said, "On my seventeenth birthday I shall marry a poet. And my wedding gown will be delicate lace."

Sarah was small and dark and wise, and she always carried a book in her hand. And when she looked up from her reading she said, "On my seventeenth birthday I shall marry a judge. And my wedding gown will be ivory silk."

Kate, the youngest, had curly brown hair. She spent most of her day by the stove in the kitchen. She only stopped her cooking to say, "On my seventeenth birthday I shall marry a sailor, and my wedding gown will be fine cool cotton, crisper than sea foam, and just as white."

"A sailor!" said her sisters. "A cotton gown! Oh Kate, what a strange little girl you are."

On an autumn day when the leaves were falling, the sisters' godmother came to see them. She stayed with the sisters for seven days, and before she left she gave each girl a present.

Eleanor's present was a pair of shoes. They were shining silver, with high twinkling heels.

"I shall dance in these shoes all night," said Eleanor.

Rosamund's present was a blue satin ribbon, as blue as her eyes.

"I shall wear it in my hair when I walk by the lake," said Rosamund.

Sarah's present was an old, wise book. It was big and heavy, and bound in leather.

"I shall sit beneath an oak tree to read it," said Sarah.

Kate's present was a big brown cooking pot.

"What shall I cook in it?" said Kate.

The godmother smiled at Kate, and said, "Cook whatever it smells of, my dear."

The other three sisters laughed, and said, "Oh, Kate, a cooking pot! What a strange present."

Kate put the pot on a shelf, and forgot it.

A year passed. Then Eleanor put on her finest dress, and her silver shoes with the twinkling high heels, and she went to a ball. A prince fell in love with the tall fair Eleanor, who danced so proudly in the silver shoes. On her seventeenth birthday she married her prince, wearing a gown of shining silver.

Another year passed. Rosamund took the blue satin ribbon and wore it in her hair as she walked by the lake. A poet stood by the edge of the lake, looking down at the still blue water. And then he looked up and saw blue, blue eyes, and the ribbon that matched them in Rosamund's hair. And the poet fell in love with Rosamund. On her seventeenth birthday she married her poet, wearing a gown of delicate lace.

At the end of yet another year, Sarah took the old, wise book, and sat beneath an oak tree to read it. A judge passed by on his way to the city, and when he saw the small, solemn Sarah, her head bent over the big old book, he fell in love with her. When Sarah's seventeenth birthday came, she married her judge, wearing ivory silk.

Then Kate was alone, dreaming of her sailor.

As day followed day she grew lonely and sad. She had no one to talk to except a robin that perched on the kitchen windowsill.

"When will my sailor come?" she asked him. "Will he *ever* come? Tell me, robin."

But the robin couldn't answer, and as week followed week, Kate grew more and more lonely and forlorn. And then, one day, she remembered the cooking pot. She took it down from the kitchen shelf, and she seemed to hear her godmother saying, "Cook whatever it smells of, my dear."

"It smells of nothing at all," said Kate.

She took the big brown cooking pot and walked

down the lane with it, holding it carefully. Presently a farmer came riding on his horse.

"Tell me," said Kate. "What shall I cook in this big brown cooking pot?"

The farmer took it in his strong brown hands.

"Cook whatever it smells of," he said. "Good red beef and rich brown gravy."

Kate went farther along the lane and came to a cottage with a garden at the front. A very old lady was sitting in the doorway.

"Tell me," said Kate. "What shall I cook in this big brown cooking pot?"

The old lady took it in her tiny old hands.

"Cook whatever it smells of," she said. "Caraway and parsley and bay leaves and thyme."

Kate went farther along the lane, and she came to a garden where a strong young man was whistling to himself as he hoed the soil.

"Tell me," said Kate. "What shall I cook in this big brown cooking pot?"

The young man took it in his earthy hands.

"Cook whatever it smells of," he said. "Onions and potatoes and carrots and beans."

Kate went back along the lane to the kitchen, and she still didn't know about the big brown cooking pot.

"Tell me, robin," she said. "Who was right?"

But the robin couldn't answer, and he flew away.

"Perhaps all three of them were right," said Kate.

So she filled the big brown cooking pot with good red beef and rich brown gravy, and caraway and parsley and bay leaves and thyme, and onions and potatoes and carrots and beans. And she put it in the stove to cook very slowly.

An hour went by, and the bright little kitchen was filled with the rich warm smell of cooking. Kate sat waiting by the open window, while the hot stew bubbled in the big brown pot.

"And there's no one to eat it but me," she said. "Tell me, robin, when will he come?"

Over the hill a mile away, walking with long firm strides he came. He was young and tall, with a sailor's steady eyes, and the quiet strength of a sailor about him. He had nowhere to go, no home of his own. So, back from the sea, he walked on the hills, enjoying the feel of the springing grass, and the smell of the earth and the wind and the trees. Then the sailor suddenly lifted his head. It wasn't the earth he could smell, or the trees, or the cold salty tang of the lonely sea. The sailor stopped, and looked around him. Then with long firm strides he walked down the hill.

In the bright little kitchen, Kate looked up. And

there in the doorway stood a tall young sailor. He looked at Kate with his steady blue eyes.

"I'm home," he said. "I'm home from the sea."

On her seventeenth birthday Kate married her sailor. And her wedding gown was fine cool cotton, crisper than sea foam, and just as white.

The Prettybeetle

Ｗ WHEN MORNING came the sun rose over the garden. And all the little flying creatures and the little creeping creatures came out of their night places. "It's a new day," they said to each other.

But Blackbeetle sat on a dandelion leaf. He said nothing.

"The sunshine is wonderful," said the butterflies to the bees.

"It's warm on our wings," said the bees to the butterflies.

But Blackbeetle stayed on his dandelion leaf and said nothing.

But he thought: "When the sun shines on *me*, I'm just black, like the night."

Bee flew over the dandelion plant, and his fuzzy round body was the color of toffee, and his wings were like shining silk.

"He's pretty," said Blackbeetle.

Caterpillar came past the dandelion plant, looping and hooping his soft yellow body.

"Pretty!" said Blackbeetle.

Then Ladybird skimmed over Blackbeetle's head, her wings gleaming red.

"She's pretty too," Blackbeetle said. "But *I'm* just black, the color of night."

Out of the house and into the garden came a little girl. Her name was Jenny. She came down the steps and onto the lawn.

Bee flew past, and Jenny watched him.

"Hello, toffee-bee," she said. "You're pretty."

Then Caterpillar came, looping and hooping, and Jenny knelt on the grass to watch him.

"You're pretty," she said. "Fat yellow caterpillar."
Then Ladybird fluttered along in the sunshine.

"Ladybird, ladybird, fly away home," said Jenny, "You're a pretty red ladybird."

Blackbeetle sat on his dandelion leaf, and Jenny didn't see him. She said to herself, "I think I'll paint a picture, with all sorts of colors." And she went indoors to fetch her paint box.

"All sorts of colors," Blackbeetle said. "Like toffee-colored bee, and yellow caterpillar, and red ladybird. Jenny says they're pretty, but she wouldn't call *me* pretty. I'm just black."

Blackbeetle sat on his dandelion plant, feeling sorry for himself. Then he began to *think*. He would make himself a color, that's what he'd do. Blackbeetle walked off the dandelion plant, across the lawn to the flower bed. He stopped at the bottom of a snapdragon plant and looked up and up at the bright red flowers. Bumblebee was up there, but you could only see the back of him. The front of him was hidden inside a flower. And when he came out, he was yellow. He was covered all over with dusty yellow pollen.

Blackbeetle said, "I'll do that. Then I'll be a yellowbeetle."

Up he climbed, up and up the stalk. It was dark inside the snapdragon flower, and the pollen made him

feel tickly inside. But when he came out, he was yellow. He climbed down the stalk and sat on the grass. Now he was a yellowbeetle.

And then—Blackbeetle started to sneeze. *Achee, achee! Achiff, achiff!* The tickle inside him sneezed itself out. And when he had sneezed a dozen times, the pollen had all been shaken off. Now he was just plain black again.

"Oh bother!" said Blackbeetle. "I must try something else."

Away he went to the water butt. The water inside was green in the summer. Blackbeetle had seen it once. Up he climbed to the top of the water butt. Then he looked carefully over the edge. Far down, down in the darkness, the water was green and soft and bubbly. Blackbeetle breathed very deeply, then he dived. The coldness closed round his body, and the wet green bubbles clung to his back. Then slowly he clambered out of the water, up to the top of the butt again, down the outside, and onto the grass.

He sat there feeling pleased with himself. Now he was a greenbeetle.

And then—Blackbeetle started to shiver. He had never felt so cold in his life. And as he shivered—for two whole minutes—the dark green bubbles slid off his back. Now, once more, he was just plain black.

"Oh bother!" said Blackbeetle. "I must think of something else."

But before he had time to do any thinking, Jenny came into the garden again. She sat down on the bottom step, and beside her she arranged a jam jar of water, a paint box, a paint brush and a big sheet of paper.

"What shall I paint?" she said to herself. "Something pretty, with lots of colors. Oh bother! I've forgotten to bring out my paint rag. Never mind, I'll use this old blue handkerchief."

Jenny started to paint a picture, but she didn't like it. She washed her brush in the jam jar of water, and wiped it clean on the old blue handkerchief. Then she spread out the handkerchief flat on the grass to dry in the sunshine.

Blackbeetle said, "If I sat on that nice little blue carpet, if I sat in the middle of it long enough, I might turn blue. Then I'd be a bluebeetle."

Blackbeetle walked right onto the handkerchief and sat quite still in the middle.

Jenny had started to paint again, but she still didn't like the picture she was making. She washed her brush in the jam jar of water, and stretched out a hand toward the old blue handkerchief. Blackbeetle didn't have time to walk off it. Jenny suddenly picked it up and Blackbeetle was tossed into the air. Then down he fell, quite bewildered, right into Jenny's paint box. He landed very hard with a thick wet plop on his back in the brightest of the bright red paint.

Jenny looked at his waggling legs. Then very carefully she picked him up and set him gently beside her on the step.

"Poor beetle," she said. "You're all red."

But she didn't say he was pretty.

The paint was slimy on Blackbeetle's back, and it smelled very nasty.

"Never mind," said Jenny. "I'll wipe it all off."

She wiped all over Blackbeetle's back with a corner of the old blue handkerchief.

Then she said, "Goodness, you aren't black at all. You're all sorts of colors, shiny ones. You're blue, and green, and yellow, and mauve, and the colors go away and then they come back. You're pretty."

Blackbeetle felt the sun on his back, and a warm, wonderful happiness inside him.

"Don't go away," Jenny told him. "I want to paint you. I'll start with blue. Now I'll use some green— dark green, like moss. And yellow, and mauve. There! I've finished. You can look."

Carefully, Blackbeetle stepped on the paper. Then slowly he walked around the picture, looking at the colors. They were beautiful.

"I *told* you how pretty you were," said Jenny. "You're a prettybeetle. That's what you are—a prettybeetle."

Blackbeetle walked across the lawn. He was very happy.

"The sunshine is wonderful," he said to the butterflies. "It's warm on my back, and it's wonderful."

Mousie Guitar

THE MOUSIE FAMILY lived in a larder, in the big old kitchen of a farmhouse.

There was Mousie Mama, and Mousie Papa, and Mousie aunts, and Mousie uncles. There were little Mousie children too, by the dozen, and they squeaked and squabbled and giggled and scuttled. All except one, and he was different. He played the guitar.

On weekdays he played it softly to himself, in whatever quiet corner he could find. But on Saturday nights the whole Mousie family gathered together on the larder shelves, and Mousie Guitar sat on the bread bin and played his guitar while everyone sang.

Then Uncle Ebenezer came to stay with the Mousie family for three whole weeks. Uncle Ebenezer lived in the town. He was stout and elderly and very, very strict. The little Mousie children called him Mousie Strict Uncle.

"You must all behave properly," said Mousie Mama. "You must try to squeak softly, and you mustn't squabble. And Mousie Guitar, you mustn't play music. Your Uncle Ebenezer doesn't like music."

Mousie Papa took the little guitar and put it away in an empty matchbox. And he took the matchbox into the kitchen and hid it high on the saucepan shelf, in the big brown stewpot that no one ever used.

Next day, Uncle Ebenezer arrived. The Mousie children whispered in a corner, "Hush! Mousie Strict Uncle is here!"

The rest of the week passed very slowly. Mousie Guitar sang softly to himself in whatever quiet corner he could find. The singing seemed to help him a little. But on Saturday night he could bear it no longer. The Mousie grown-ups were gathered in the larder, talking politely to Mousie Strict Uncle, and the little Mousie children were sitting in a row with their paws neatly folded, waiting for their supper.

Mousie Guitar crept quietly away and went to explore the big brown cupboard that stood in the corner by the kitchen cooker.

On the bottom shelf there were piles of old newspapers, and a teapot lid and a rusty old knife. And right in the corner was an empty baked bean tin.

"That will come in useful," said Mousie Guitar.

The second shelf of the big brown cupboard was full of pots of marmalade and jars of bottled plums. And right in the corner was a jam-pot cover.

"And it's just the right size," said Mousie Guitar.

The third shelf was piled high with cups and saucers, and dinner plates, and tea plates, and big brown teapots. And right in the corner was a little white egg cup.

"And it's just the right height," said Mousie Guitar.

There were wooden boxes up on the fourth shelf, with teaspoons in them, and a big curly corkscrew. And right in the corner were two wooden skewers.

"Just what I need," said Mousie Guitar.

He picked up the tin and the jam-pot cover and the little white egg cup and the two wooden skewers. And he took them all to the top of the cupboard. Then he fixed the round white jam-pot cover over the empty end of the tin, and beat on it gently with his paw: *Tumarum.*

"It's a beautiful drum I have," he said.

Then he picked up the skewers and sat on the egg cup and played on the drum with all his might.

Tumarum, tumarum, tumarum arap,
Rumpadiddle, rumpadiddle,
Tum tum tum.

Down in the larder Mousie Strict Uncle pricked up his ears.

"What's that?" he said.

Mousie Papa's face was as black as a thundercloud, and Mousie Mama looked at him anxiously.

"Papa will stop it at once," she said. "It's the people upstairs in the parlor I expect. They're dancing, dear Uncle. Now, let me make you a nice cup of tea, and Papa will stop that dreadful noise."

While Mousie Mama made a cup of tea, Mousie Papa hurried to the kitchen. And there on top of the big brown cupboard was Mousie Guitar, sitting on an egg cup, playing his drum for all he was worth.

"Stop it at once," shouted Mousie Papa. "And go to bed without any supper."

Mousie Guitar scuttled away, and when he was in bed he cried himself to sleep.

The second week of Mousie Strict Uncle's visit passed very, very slowly indeed. Mousie Guitar whistled to himself, all alone in a quiet corner. The whistling seemed to cheer him a little, but by Saturday night he could bear it no longer.

The Mousie family were gathered in the larder, and Mousie Guitar crept quietly away and went to explore the five little cupboards between the cooker and the kitchen sink.

In the first cupboard there was a shopping basket, and some paper bags, and an old woollen glove. And right at the back, a tiny yellow bottle with a label that said: "Vanilla Essence."

"That will come in useful," said Mousie Guitar, and he picked it up and put it on the draining board.

In the second cupboard there were shiny round cake tins, and two silver toast racks, and a wooden spoon. And right at the back—a small empty medicine bottle.

"And it's just the right size," said Mousie Guitar.

He took the bottle to the draining board and put it beside the Vanilla Essence bottle.

In the third cupboard there was dust on the floor, and a wrinkled potato growing long white stalks. And right at the back, covered with cobwebs, was an empty, middle-sized olive oil bottle.

"It's exactly right," said Mousie Guitar.

And he took the bottle to the draining board and put it beside the small medicine bottle.

In the fourth cupboard there were kitchen scales, an old enamel jug, and a packet of spaghetti. And right at the back—a large sauce bottle.

"It couldn't be better," said Mousie Guitar, and he took the bottle to the draining board and put it beside the olive oil bottle.

In the fifth cupboard there were jars of chutney, and pickled onions, and beetroot in vinegar. And right at the back—a little silver mustard spoon.

"Just what I needed," said Mousie Guitar, and he took the spoon to the draining board, where the four empty bottles stood in a row. Then Mousie Guitar ran along the draining board, holding the mustard spoon tight in his paw. And he played on the bottles with all his might.

Ping ping, tinkle-tinkle, dingalong dong,
Dong dong dingaling, tinkle-tinkle ping.

Down in the larder Mousie Strict Uncle pricked up his ears.

"What's that?" he said.

Mousie Papa's face was as black as a thundercloud, and Mousie Mama looked at him anxiously.

"Papa will stop it at once," she said. "It's the church bells ringing I expect, dear Uncle. Now, let me make you some nice hot soup, and Papa will stop that dreadful noise."

While Mousie Mama made some soup, Mousie Papa hurried to the kitchen. And there on the draining board was Mousie Guitar, running up and down with the mustard spoon, and playing on the bottles for all he was worth.

"Stop it at once!" shouted Mousie Papa. "And go to bed without any supper."

Mousie Guitar scuttled away, and when he was in bed he cried himself to sleep.

The third week of Mousie Strict Uncle's visit seemed as though it would never end. Mousie Guitar sat in a corner, and now and again there were tears in his eyes. By Saturday night he could bear it no longer, and he went to explore the saucepan shelf.

There were five things standing in a row on the shelf. A middle-sized saucepan, an earthenware casserole, a double boiler, a frying pan, and a big brown stewpot that no one ever used.

Mousie Guitar sat in the saucepan and sang to himself, softly and sadly. Then he scuttled into the earthenware casserole, and walked all round it, whistling quietly. The double boiler had a lid on top, so Mousie Guitar sat on the handle, humming a little tune to himself. Then he sat in the frying pan, trying not to cry. The big brown stewpot that no one ever used was deep and dark, a place for hiding. Mousie Guitar scuttled inside it, and sat there rubbing his eyes with his paws, trying to push back the tears that kept coming.

Then suddenly he found he was sitting on a matchbox. The matchbox had something inside it. It rattled. Mousie Guitar looked inside and there, quite safe, was his little guitar.

Down in the pantry Mousie Strict Uncle pricked up his ears.

"What's that?" he said.

Up in the stewpot a happy little Mousie smiled to himself as he played the guitar.

Plink-plank, ripple-ripple, twink-twink-
twang,
Twinkle-twinkle, ripple-ripple, plink-plink-
plang.

Then Mousie Mama found her voice at last.

"Oh, Uncle Ebenezer," she said. "Dear Uncle, Mousie Papa will stop it at once. I expect it's the . . . well, perhaps it's the. . . ."

"Water in the stream," said Mousie Strict Uncle, and suddenly his eyes were full of dreams. "It's like water rippling over smooth gray pebbles. Or a cool breeze singing in the branches of the elms. Or the twinkle of the stars in the dark night sky."

Surprised Mousie eyes stared at Uncle Ebenezer. Then Mousie Papa recovered himself and looked across proudly at Mousie Mama.

"Oh, Uncle Ebenezer," said Mousie Mama. "It's none of those things you said, dear Uncle. It's our own little son and he's playing his guitar."

It seemed like a dream to Mousie Guitar. He remembered the confusion in the kitchen, and the smiling, and all the little Mousies chattering at once. He remembered looking at Mousie Strict Uncle, and Mousie Strict Uncle was saying, "Well done! A beautiful sound! Quite, quite beautiful!"

145

Then Mousie Mama was hugging him, and Mousie Papa was patting his head, and suddenly all of them were back in the larder, and every Mousie face was turned toward him—smiling.

Then Mousie Guitar sat on the bread bin and played his guitar while everyone sang.

146

"More!" cried Mousie Strict Uncle. "More!"

Then Mousie Guitar played again and again, till the stars came out in the dark night sky and the great round moon shone bright and yellow.

One-two-three-four, Hoppity and Nost

∽ ONCE UPON A TIME there were three little creatures called One-two-three-four, Hoppity and Nost, and none of them was bigger than a lump of sugar.

One-two-three-four had four little legs.

Hoppity had one leg.

And Nost had wings.

The three of them lived beneath the edge of a roof, in a dusty old bird's nest belonging to a swallow who had long since flown away to the South. Every morning when the sun came up One-two-three-four, Hoppity and Nost slid down the drainpipe and played in the dustbin, and they never, never went anywhere else.

But one special morning when they slid down the drainpipe Reddips was just coming up through the drain. Reddips had eight legs and always walked backwards. He stood on the grating and stared very rudely at One-two-three-four, Hoppity and Nost.

"Oh, it's you," he said. "The three little friends. I suppose you're going to the dustbin as usual. You never go anywhere else, do you?"

"How do you know?" said One-two-three-four.

"We might go *miles* away," said Hoppity.

"Miles and miles and miles," said Nost.

Reddips laughed at them. He laughed so much that he curled right up and fell through the grating. One-two-three-four, Hoppity and Nost didn't like being laughed at—not at all. They put their faces close to the grating and shouted, "We *are* going somewhere, so there!"

"Miles away," said One-two-three-four.

"On an expedition," Hoppity said.

"To Africa," said Nost.

Reddips' voice was a watery echo coming up from the deep black drain: "There are snakes in Africa. And tigers too. You have to beat at the snakes with a stick, and if you see a tiger you run for your lives."

Reddips' laughter echoed round the drain.

"Anyway, you're only going to the dustbin. You have to go over the sea to Africa, and over a mountain, and into the jungle."

One-two-three-four, Hoppity and Nost didn't like being laughed at—not at all. They decided to set off for Africa at once. But first they put their faces close to the grating and shouted down the drain, "Silly old Reddips. We *are* going to Africa. *You* needn't laugh, you'd be frightened of a patterkiller, silly old Reddips, or even a cabbytat. *We* aren't frightened."

Then they washed their faces and set off for Africa.

Halfway down the garden they came to a puddle.

"Look, it's the sea!" said One-two-three-four.

"It's big," said Hoppity.

"And deep," said Nost.

Then One-two-three-four crossed the sea on his four little legs, *splash, splash, gurgle-glug.*

Hoppity crossed on his one little leg, *plosh, plosh, plosh.*

And Nost flew, *flutter, flutter, flit.*

When they landed on the other side they looked around them.

"Africa is big," said One-two-three-four.

"With snakes," said Hoppity.

"And tigers," said Nost.

Farther down the garden they came to a flower-pot.

"Look, it's the mountain," said One-two-three-four.

"It's high," said Hoppity.

"And steep," said Nost.

Then One-two-three-four climbed the mountain on his four little legs, *tipper, tapper, heave.*

Hoppity climbed on his one little leg, *tap, tap, heave, tap, tap, heave.*

And Nost flew, *flutter, flutter, flit.*

They looked all around them for snakes and fierce tigers. But there weren't any showing, so on they went.

At the bottom of the garden they came to a cabbage patch.

"Look, it's the jungle," said One-two-three-four.

"It's dark," said Hoppity.

"And dangerous," said Nost.

It was damp and dark, down among the cabbage stalks.

"We must camp for the night," said One-two-three-four.

"We must put up a tent," Hoppity said.

"At once," said Nost.

They found a big round cabbage leaf and made it into a little green tent, and they propped it up with a stick for a tent pole. Then they all lay down and got ready to sleep.

Over the top of the cabbage leaf, slither and slide, came a long yellow caterpillar. It came to the edge of the leaf and looked over. One-two-three-four, Hoppity and Nost saw a great slidey yellow thing hanging from their roof.

"Look, it's a snake," said One-two-three-four.

"Help, we must beat it with a stick," said Hoppity.

"Quick!" said Nost.

Then they all caught hold of the tent pole stick and pulled it toward them, and the tent fell down. By the time they had wriggled themselves from beneath it, the great yellow slidey thing had disappeared from sight.

"We frightened him away," said One-two-three-four.

"*We* weren't frightened," Hoppity said.

"Not at all," said Nost.

152

They put up their tent again and settled down to sleep.

Then down the garden came a green-eyed tabby cat. He stalked through the cabbage patch hunting for a mouse, and when he saw the leaf-tent he wondered what it was. So he put his head down close to the ground and looked through a little ragged hole in the leaf.

One-two-three-four, Hoppity and Nost saw a great green eye at the door of their tent.

"Look, it's a tiger," said One-two-three-four.

"Help, we must run for our lives," said Hoppity.

"Oh, my goodness!" said Nost.

But suddenly their legs and their wings went wobbly, and they shook so much that they couldn't move an inch. Then a voice from somewhere said: "Supper time, pussycat." And the tiger said, "Miaow," and disappeared.

"He was *easily* frightened," said One-two-three-four.

"Tigers aren't terrible," Hoppity said.

"Not terrible at all," said Nost.

Then the three of them slept for the rest of the night and when morning came they set off for home, over the mountain and over the sea.

"So we've been to Africa," said One-two-three-four.

"Reddips won't believe us," Hoppity said.

"Never," said Nost.

Reddips was just coming up from the drain.

He stared very rudely at One-two-three-four, Hoppity and Nost. And then he said, "Oh, it's you again. The three little friends. I suppose you've been playing in the dustbin as usual."

"As a matter of fact," said One-two-three-four, "we've been on an expedition to Africa."

"We frightened a long yellow snake," said Hoppity.

"Not to mention a tiger," said Nost.

Then Reddips laughed so much that he shook. And he shook so much that he shook himself to pieces. And all the little pieces fell through the grating.

One-two-three-four, Hoppity and Nost put their faces close to the grating and stared down into the deep black drain.

"Poor old Reddips," they said. "Poor Reddips. We frightened him to pieces. Poor old Reddips."

Then One-two-three-four, Hoppity and Nost went to the dustbin and played there, all day.